0d2a

The Amethyst Ring

Also by Scott O'Dell

The Black Pearl
The Captive
Carlota
Child of Fire
The Cruise of the Arctic Star
The Dark Canoe
The Feathered Serpent
The Hawk That Dare Not Hunt by Day
Island of the Blue Dolphins
Journey to Jericho
Kathleen, Please Come Home
The King's Fifth
Sarah Bishop
Sing Down the Moon
The Spanish Smile
The 290
Zia

The Amethyst Ring

Scott O'Dell

Houghton Mifflin Company Boston 1983

RETA E. KING LIBRARY
CHADRON STATE COLLEGE
CHADRON, NE 69337

O'Dell, Scott, 1903-
The amethyst ring.

Summary: Spanish seminarian Julián Escobar, known to the Mayas as Lord Kukulcán and worshipped as a god, witnesses the fall of the Mayan and Incan civilizations with the coming of Cortés and Pizarro.
[1. Mayas — Fiction. 2. Incas — Fiction. 3. Indians of Mexico — Fiction. 4. Indians of South America — Fiction. 5. Latin America — History — To 1600 — Fiction]
I. Title.
PZ7.0237Am 1983 [Fic] 82-23388
ISBN 0-395-33886-7

Copyright © 1983 by Scott O'Dell

All rights reserved. No part of this work may be reproduced or transmitted in any form or by any means, electronic or mechanical, including photocopying and recording, or by any information storage or retrieval system, except as may be expressly permitted by the 1976 Copyright Act or in writing from the publisher. Requests for permission should be addressed in writing to Houghton Mifflin Company, 2 Park Street, Boston, Massachusetts 02108.

Printed in the United States of America
V 10 9 8 7 6 5 4 3 2 1

For Elizabeth

Author's Note

The Amethyst Ring is the third book of a chronicle based upon the legend of Kukulcán, god of the Maya, who came to Yucatán during the ninth century A.D. Kukulcán was not born a god but became one because of his humble and compassionate life. For several centuries he ruled over the great nation of the Maya, then mysteriously disappeared, promising to return.

In *The Captive,* the first book of this chronicle, Julián Escobar, a young Spanish seminarian, is cast away among the Maya and by chance and cunning assumes the guise of the returning god.

The Feathered Serpent continues his story, first with the Maya and then the Aztéca, during the days when Hernán Cortés and a few hundred soldiers conquered the mighty emperor Moctezuma, who could summon an army of a million warriors with one blast from a conch shell horn.

The Amethyst Ring follows the fortunes of Kukulcán, Lord of the Wind of Knives, after he leaves the Maya and joins Francisco Pizarro in the land of the Inca.

The ancient Incan city of Machu Picchu, with its secret Temple of the Sun, was never discovered by Pizarro. It was first seen some three hundred years later by an American explorer.

Francisco Pizarro, who killed tens of thousands of Indians during his conquest of fabulous Peru, was himself killed by a band of his enemies. Old and ill, he was surprised in his palace, fought his attackers from room to room, and only died by odd mischance, sword in hand. His body lies today in the city of Lima, in a small crystal casket. A wizened little man scarcely more than five feet tall, he has the puzzled face of a marmoset.

The Amethyst Ring

•

Once again, lest it be forgot, I swear in the name of our holy apostle St. Peter, by the bronze horse of Toledo, by the six blind bishops of Valladolid, in the name of Kukulcán, Knight of the Red Jaguar, that what I write here is the truth, as I see it.

A *chubasco* struck us before we left the highlands. For two days the wind slowed our horses to a shambling walk. The rain drummed upon our armor like hunter's shot. Yet, except for brief evening prayer and fitful sleep, we never chose to halt until the storm blew away, and the sun's first shadow fell upon the coast of Yucatán.

We were on a narrow trail, trending downward along the face of a cliff toward a lagoon whose banks were lined with palm trees. Beyond their borders lay the sea, dull gray in the half-light before dawn.

At the sun's first glimmer, I roused myself to say in a shivering voice, "Let us pause, *amigo,* and give thanks. Now that danger lies behind us."

"Danger," snorted the dwarf, slipping down from his dappled mare. "Danger! It still lies around us everywhere. In front of us. On all sides. In all directions."

"Also, my friend, in our very bones. We have eaten it. Breathed it."

"Bones?" The dwarf gave the word a scornful ring. "I have none. My bones became jelly long since."

"Since that morning high priest Chalco left us standing in the square," I said. "With the wind crawling up our legs."

"Ayee, and never came back. The *bastarde. El bastarde loco* never showed his ugly face again."

"Likewise when Moctezuma curled his thin lips and said to me, 'Do you believe that the warrior who takes a prisoner and then watches him die upon the altar should know that sooner or later he will follow him into the hereafter by the same kind of death? That he should say to this man, "Today it is you, tomorrow it is me."' And went on to describe the Aztéca heaven — flowers bloom everywhere, butterflies dart about, happy warriors fight mock battles with mock weapons under cloudless skies, while fountains play and singers sing like little birds."

"I greatly prefer our Spanish hell to the Aztéca heaven," the dwarf said.

"We will likely have some of both long before this is over," I said.

We could joke now. In the dawn's light we could smile grimly at each other about things we had barely mentioned before, and then only in whispers born of fear.

"All of it happened fast, like a bad dream," the dwarf said. "Like a nightmare. Dante could write a great poem about it. If I see him — and the chances are excellent that I will — I'll present him with the details."

"There are many," I said. "Many to sort out, the good from the bad, the useful from those of no use."

"May God grant you the time to do so," the dwarf said.

In truth, I had done little else from the hour when we left Don Luis de Arroyo dead at the foot of the temple, his heart removed, and Hernán Cortés crouching at a skimpy fire, licking the wounds he had suffered that night at the hands of the Aztéca — little else as we fled for our lives through wind and rain than digest the horrible events of the past.

There was nothing wrong with the idea of making a journey to the capital city of the Aztéca, there to learn from Moctezuma himself how his country was organized and run. I had seen much, I had absorbed much, during my months in Tenochtitlán. My head was crammed with ideas, some new, some as old as Rome. And of these, one was overriding. The Aztéca nation was based upon power and flourished because of it. With one single blast on a conch-shell horn Moctezuma could summon half a million warriors to his side. Cities and towns and villages trembled at his name, even his shadow. They paid him tribute in full measure and on time, whether the harvest was good or not good, on pain of destruction and death.

And then, overnight, as Hernán Cortés marched into the city, the scene changed. The world turned upside down. Most of what I had learned I had learned for naught. The mighty emperor whom I had come to observe, perhaps even to make an alliance with, to copy, was dead, dead at the hands of his own people.

"Señor," I said to the dwarf, who was busy inspecting the ropes that secured the sacks that held a fortune in gold, which he did every hour or two, "señor, our task when we reach the island, if by chance we do, will be to stop digging in the jungle for lost temples and lost cities. We start at once upon fortifications to save the city we have."

"That," said the dwarf, "or set our sails for home, for Seville, that marvelous city of perpetual spring beside the silvery Guadalquivir, hopes and dreams fulfilled."

"You will see much," I said, "before you ever see Seville again."

The dawn brightened on the lip of the sea. On the trail below an odd-shaped tree caught my eye. It was growing in a crevice without any sign of earth to support it, most of its roots exposed and clinging to the rock. The trunk had been shaped by the wind and grew to the height of my horse's back. A tortured limb, covered with sharp thorns, branched out on each side of the trunk near the top, and this is what gave the tree an odd appearance, the perfect form of a cross.

I reined in the stallion. "Let's pause, Don Guillermo. Let's take a decent moment to give thanks to Her who has brought us here. Perhaps more than a moment, now that the danger has lessened."

I knelt before the cruciform tree, the dwarf kneeling beside me, and we prayed together, reciting the litany. But as the sun rose out of the sea, he took a thorn from one of the branches and pricked his thumb. The drop of blood he held up to the sun. It glistened like a jewel.

He handed the thorn to me, surprised that I did not hesitate to use it and then to hold my bleeding finger to the sun.

"God fashioned the sun," I said. "He set it in place and started it moving majestically through the heavens. All life comes from the sun. Nothing lives without it, not even the blind creatures in the dark caverns of the sea. The sun is God's creation. God, in one of His many forms, is the sun. It is proper to greet the sun after its long journey through the night and the gates of hell. The sun is exhausted and needs strength."

"It is said in the Book, 'Thou shalt not make unto thee any graven image.' "

"The sun is not graven," I said, "and not an image."

"You have given the matter thought, I observe," the dwarf said. "And I am in agreement. God is everywhere. Even in me."

He laughed his croaking early-morning laugh and tapped his chest, where, if by chance he had a soul, it might reside.

"And the devil likewise," the dwarf said.

He had lost some weight during the past dreadful days, but still he looked much the same as he had that morning on the beach, a lump with two legs and two long arms. If the devil was not just an emanation, if the devil had a true and recognizable shape, then he would appear exactly in the shape of Guillermo Cantú.

"Tell me," he said, "how you feel about this subject of human sacrifice. Now that you have been among the mighty Aztéca."

"How I felt before, my friend. It is an abomination."

"What about the sacrifice of animals — monkeys, peccaries, deer — instead of humans?"

"I am against this also."

"But not the pricking of the finger?"

"No, the blood on your finger belongs to you. It comes from your own veins."

"Yes, it comes from there. Consequently, it belongs to the donor, to the one who gives it. But do you think it really strengthens the sun?"

"It strengthens those who give the blood. That is important."

The dwarf pondered, one eye on the mare that carried the sacks crammed with gold. "I wonder," he said, "how the Consistory would look upon this."

"The priests of the Consistory sit far away across the seas," I said, "in comfort, never having met an Indian nor heard a *maman* drum nor mindless thousands shouting their wild, spine-freezing chants."

I was standing with my hand raised to the brightening coast when a party of Maya came up the trail from that direction. Without speaking, they paused at the cruciform tree, choosing its thorns carefully.

After all had given their salutations to the sun, one of them said to me, "You are a white man. Where do you come from?"

"From Tenochtitlán."

"My name is Xacal and I hear of fighting in that city," he said. "We have salt to sell. Should we go to Tenochtitlán to sell it?"

"Sell it in Cholólan," I said. "Or some other place. There's trouble in Tenochtitlán."

"Trouble in Ixtlilzochitl also," he said, pointing toward the east. "There."

"People dead in the lagoon," said a young man who had Xacal's yellow, close-set eyes and appeared to be his son. "Many people dead."

Ixtlilzochitl was the trading center where the *Santa Margarita* lay anchored, at least when we had left her.

I drew a picture of the caravel, using my finger in the dirt. "A big canoe," I said to the boy. "In the lagoon beyond the river. Have you seen it?"

"Two," he said.

"Two big canoes?"

"Two," his father said and drew a picture beside mine. "Two big canoes."

"Which means that the *Santa Margarita* is still there," the dwarf said. "The dead men mean that there's been fighting."

"Did you see the white men fighting?" I asked Xacal.

He cupped his ear, indicating he had only heard of it. I pressed him for other details, but I had difficulty with his dialect and learned little more except that loud noises and black smoke came out of the ships and that one of them had a hole in its side.

Eyeing the mare that carried the dwarf's gold, Xacal said, "Are you *pochtéca*?" and before I could answer, "What do you trade? I see gold on the back of the animal. Do you like salt? Everybody likes salt. We trade."

He spoke softly, but underneath lay a threat. One of the party tapped the sack with his cudgel. The sack held a temple bell, which gave off a lively ring. The man tapped the sack once more. Again the bell rang. He glanced at the dwarf and then at me, measuring us. We were white men with a load of gold.

Before the bell stopped ringing, we were in the saddles, moving off down the trail, the three mares close behind. Shouts and rocks flew after us. We did not look back.

Before long we came to the place where we had hidden our ceremonial attire and changed into *pochtéca* garb for the journey to Tenochtitlán months before. Everything of mine was in good shape, the quetzal plumes as beautiful as ever. However, I had left my mask on the *Santa Margarita* and had to borrow Cantú's, a jaguar mask with a sneering mouth and red fangs. I would have preferred to wear the elaborate mask decorated with turquoise, emeralds, and gold that Chalco the high priest had hidden, but we couldn't find it.

"He's come this way and picked it up," the dwarf said.

"Somebody has. Indians likely."

"If Indians took it, they would have taken my mask also."

The dwarf fared less well with his clothes. Yet, elated that at last we were within two short leagues of Ixtlilzochitl, he failed to notice that something with sharp teeth had nibbled on his rear feathers.

We rode hard toward the coast under a hot sun, through clouds of stinging insects.

• •

We found the *Santa Margarita* riding safely at anchor in the lagoon, not far from where she lay when we began our journey to Tenochtitlán. The second caravel, oddly named *Delfín Azul* — the one the Indian trader had described — sat on a sandbar a quarter of a mile away, listing to port, the morning sun shining into a broad hole in her side.

Flint Knife, the *nacom,* had spied us from afar. Black and yellow flags flew from our masts — ones I had never seen before, apparently made while we were away. As the longboat bore us across the lagoon, a shot rang out from the ship, followed by a second shot, a series of shots that passed harmlessly over our heads. Flutes, rattles, and drums set up a horrendous clatter.

Flint Knife was on his knees to greet me. Behind him, painted in all colors, bedecked in bangles and feathers, the crew lay prone as I came aboard; with wild mutterings they pressed their faces against the deck.

"It was a ghost we saw on the shore," the young *nacom* said, sobbing between words. "We thought you dead. I could not believe my eyes when I saw you get down from the horse there on the shore." He paused, overcome. "Everyone believed Chalco when he told us that you were sacrificed in Tenochtitlán by the emperor Moctezuma. Everyone except me. I clung to hope."

"Chalco brought news that I was dead?"

"Sacrificed as a tribute to the war god. He described how brave you were as you lay there on the altar and the knife descended."

"When did you see him?"

"He came after the rains. With dozens of Aztéca carrying jars of *tecuítcal,* the green moss. He wheedled me into taking him to the City of the Seven Serpents and then tried to keep me there, but I slipped away in the night."

The *nacom* paused, overcome once more. I think he would have jumped to his feet and embraced me, so great was his delight, had I not turned away. As it was, he clasped me around the knees, saying, "God of the Evening Star, Lord of the Twilight, Mighty Kukulcán, do not leave us again."

Watching some five or six paces away, but not on his knees, was a lone figure with his back against the mainmast. At first I took him to be a priest, one of the Dominicans I had seen following Cortés around during the siege in Tenochtitlán. It was possible that one of them had survived the disaster and had fled this far from the battlefield.

I adjusted the jaguar mask, which, because of its small eye holes, was difficult to see through, and cast another glance in his direction. To my surprise, a man some ten years older than I, not an elderly Dominican, confronted me.

From what I could make out, he had a forehead shaped like a turret and a jutting chin — a bigoted Spanish face as white as a fish's belly. I wondered how anyone exposed to the fierce weather of New Spain could look washed out, like a scholar after years spent among books. Yet it was not these things that held my eye. The young man was dressed in the black cassock and violet vest of a church dignitary.

A glare from the sea danced in the rigging and along the deck, changing the shape of everything. I adjusted the mask again. Neither the glare nor the mask had deceived me. No,

I was face to face with a churchman. What's more, a bishop!

Taken aback, but concealing my surprise, I asked the *nacom,* "Who is this man? Where does he come from?"

"This man," the *nacom* said, "came on the ship. It is there on the sandbar with a big hole in its side. Many warriors came also. Twenty-nine. Sixteen are dead. The others are in chains."

When the *nacom* went on to describe the battle, I turned to the bishop. As I approached him he muttered a few fervent words in Latin, as if he were fending off not just a feathered figure he had never encountered before, but the devil himself.

His words escaped me — I was surprised that my Latin had become so rusty — but they carried the unmistakable tone of authority. For a moment I was a meek seminarian, confronted by a lordly bishop. Then I recovered myself and looked hard at him through the eyeholes of my feathered mask.

"My name is Rodrigo Pedroza," the man said. "I am the Bishop-designate of the Province of Yucatán, sent hither at the instigation of the Council of the Indies, with the consent of the Governor-General of Hispaniola."

He said all this in a churchly voice, in clear, graceful Spanish, which by shaking my head I pretended not to understand. The gold *cascabeles* attached to my mask set up a clatter to bear me out.

I asked in Spanish, "Do you speak Maya?"

"No," the bishop said, "but since you are a Spaniard I don't need to." He gave me a searching look and waited for me to reply, to show some sort of emotion — surprise, consternation, guilt. When I didn't he continued, "You cannot be astounded that I know who you are. Everywhere, even in Seville, people speak of the seminarian who by chance has become a god among the savages."

He cast a scathing glance at the crew that still groveled on the deck, chanting my name; at the *nacom,* on his knees at my side. Unexpectedly, he thrust out his hands. For the first time I saw that they were bound tight with rope.

"An outrage," he said, as if he expected me to unbind him at once and fall over myself in the act. "A barbarism! Untie me."

Bishop Pedroza was accustomed to giving orders and having them obeyed. I let him stand there with his hands outstretched. From the moment I saw his black cassock and violet vest, I had made up my mind that he was an enemy. Even more of an enemy than Hernán Cortés. Cortés was an adventurer in disfavor with both the king and the Governor of Hispaniola. But Pedroza, for all I knew, had the full and far-reaching power of the Church behind him. I intended to treat him with courtesy, yet mindful that he could be a mortal adversary.

"Why should I unbind you?" I said. "You're a prisoner captured in battle. Fortunately, not dead like the others."

"Unbound, I can speak as a free man," Pedroza said.

"For a while, speak as a prisoner," I told him. "You say you're a bishop. For all I know, you might be a soldier dressed up in a bishop's garb."

Pedroza withdrew his hands. His long, white face did not change. It was as much a mask as the mask I wore.

He spoke in a quiet voice, avoiding my eyes, which stared at him through the jaguar slits.

"Whatever your role among these savages may be," he said, "whether it is Lord of the Evening Star or Rider of the Winds — I have even heard you called a god — you remain a Spaniard by birth, a subject of King Carlos the Fifth, and thereby subject to his laws. As well as to the laws and regulations of the Governor of Hispaniola, set down by him for all those who live within the boundaries of New Spain."

"On the contrary, I do live within the king's laws and the governor's regulations," I said, holding back my anger. "You do not. Otherwise you would not be a prisoner on my ship."

"The battle was an accident," the bishop said. "It happened because of a misunderstanding, which I tried to prevent and failed."

"What does he say?" the *nacom* asked.

"He says that the battle was not his fault."

"This is true. The crew of his ship learned from the Indians in the village that we carried gold. They fought hard to seize it. He could do nothing."

"Spaniards fight hard for gold," I said. "For gold first. Then for Holy Mary. Then for the king. Their lives last."

"These got no gold," the *nacom* said. "Only wounds and death."

"Good," I said. "And the ship, what is the condition of their ship? Can it be repaired?"

"Men are working now."

"How many days will they take?"

The *nacom* held up ten fingers. "Less, perhaps."

"Make it less. Half that time. We have none to lose."

Chafing his wrists against his lean stomach, Pedroza was growing very impatient with us. For a prisoner in a dangerous situation, he had an arrogant tilt to his head. There was something that he badly wanted to say, but I gave the *nacom* further instructions, all of them unnecessary, and let the bishop wait.

He writhed within his black cassock. He began to twist the large, violet-colored stone he wore on the fourth finger of his right hand — the amethyst ring of a bishop. His voice rising to a shout, he burst out with, "I carry a message of grave importance."

I let him wait a while longer. "You carry this message where?" I said at last. "In a letter? If so, bring it forth."

"I carry it in my head."

He had a huge head, long and narrow. In such a turret he could easily carry many things.

"I have a message from his honor, the Governor of Hispaniola, to Hernán Cortés," the bishop said. "It is of great urgency. If you would kindly put me onshore, I will proceed to deliver it. And may I remind you that any interference with this mission will go hard with you."

"Cortés," I said, giving the name a derisive ring, "will be difficult to find. I have just come from Tenochtitlán, where his men were slain on the causeway and drowned in the frigid waters of the lakes that surround the city. When I saw him last he was hiding among the trees, freezing beside a meager fire. Captain Cortés has no need of a message. What he needs is a new army."

The bishop's expression did not change at this, as if he had heard the news before. But he couldn't have heard it.

"By chance," I said, "this message you carry about in your head, which is a bad place for it should you be killed, does it concern Lord Kukulcán?"

"Any message from Governor Velásquez to Captain Cortés would certainly concern Kukulcán," the bishop said, omitting my title, deliberately I assumed.

"Since it does concern me," I said, "kindly let me hear it."

"The message is meant for Captain Cortés only," the bishop said.

The answer nettled me. Suspicious, I called to the *nacom*. "Search Pedroza's ship," I said. "Search every cabin and likely hiding place for letters. Have the dwarf assist you in the search. He's clever at that sort of thing."

Flint Knife set off at once in the longboat. He was gone only a short time, during which I left Pedroza and went below to make certain that the gold had not been stolen. The *nacom* and the dwarf returned with a letter addressed to Captain Cortés, sealed by a red ribbon and a daub of wax upon which Governor Velásquez had left his broad thumbprint.

"Is this the letter you were commissioned to deliver?" I asked Pedroza.

He answered by tightening his lips.

"Do you wish to read it or shall I?"

The bishop was silent.

I broke the seal and read, having some difficulty with the governor's affected flourishes, "Esteemed Captain, it has come to the attention of His Catholic Majesty the Emperor Don Carlos, and thus to me, that Julián Escobar, a native of Arroyo in Spain, has seized upon an island near the coast of Yucatán, first sighted by Admiral Grijalva, and there set himself up by various cunning devices as king. Furthermore, it is said on evidence that he has secreted an amount of gold, in excess of ten thousand ounces, upon which he has not paid the royal fifth. I suggest that at your earliest pleasure you take this Escobar into custody and deal with him as you wish. I am privy to the fact that you have said in the past, 'It would be better not to know how to write. Then one would not have to sign death sentences.' Yet I also know that with the scoundrel Montijo you displayed no mercy and had his feet removed."

"It seems," said the dwarf in his execrable Maya, "that we must put an end to this messenger who brings us threats of quick disaster."

A shadow dimmed the bishop's eyes. It told me that he had some knowledge of the Maya language and had caught the gist of Cantú's words.

"On the contrary," I said, "we should treat Bishop Pedroza with the utmost courtesy. He only brings us a message. He is not here to execute it."

I walked to the rail, tore the letter into pieces, and tossed the pieces into the sea. I did so to warn the bishop that while he was to be treated with courtesy, he was no longer protected by the laws of King Carlos and the Governor of Hispaniola. The act was not lost upon him. Pieces of the letter, a length of ribbon, floated away on the tide. Standing stiff and silent by the mainmast, he watched them disappear.

The sun shone on his violet vest. A flash of color blinded me. I suddenly remembered the words Don Luis de Arroyo had spoken on an April morning long ago. "This I promise you," he had said to me, "one day you yourself will become a bishop. As powerful as the Bishop of Burgos."

For a fleeting moment the memory was a bitter one. Then it faded in the sound of the crew's quiet chanting, "Kukulcán, Lord of the Lightning and Thunder, protect us from evil gods . . ."

"On your feet," I shouted to them. "Bring the horses on board. Put out your hands," I said to Bishop Pedroza, "and I'll unbind them."

• • •

We arrived at the Island of the Seven Serpents near evening on a day of sultry heat and tumbling clouds.

Viewed from a distance, with the sun setting, the city looked unchanged from the hour I had left it. But as we turned toward the harbor I noted that the feathered poles that marked the channel were draped in black.

The wharves and embankment were deserted. Along the thoroughfare that wound upward into the heart of the city not a light showed. The godhouse on the roof of the Temple of Kukulcán was dark. The temple itself I could not make out; it seemed a part of the falling night. The only light came from far away, murky flames that crept along the crest of St. John the Baptist, the fiery mountain. I expected to find a city in mourning, since my death at the hands of Moctezuma had been reported by high priest Chalco, but I was not prepared for the scene that now lay before me.

What adoration, what love, I must have inspired in the hearts of the people to bring them to such grief and desolation! I was overwhelmed. Tears sprang to my eyes.

Standing at the rail as we made ready to leave the ship, Bishop Pedroza announced in somber tones to no one in particular that the tales he had heard from Governor Velásquez had been misleading.

"Shining towers, such as one sees in Seville," he said, "where are they? And where the streets paved with gold?"

"In your imagination, sir," the dwarf announced. "And the governor's. This is an abandoned city that Kukulcán, Lord of the Evening Star, seeks to rebuild. A nearly impossible task."

I said nothing, satisfied that Bishop Pedroza remained unaware of the reason for the deserted streets. In due course he would discover it. Already the curious had gathered around the ship, ignorant of my presence.

When the animals were lowered to the wharf, I insisted that the bishop ride forth on one of the mares. He had never ridden a horse before and was reluctant to do so now, but I led him haltingly into the saddle and up the ramp.

As we came to the embankment, Flint Knife announced us with a blast of trumpets. The sound echoed forlornly through the silent streets. But a second blast from the conches brought people running. By the time we reached the Temple of Kukulcán, a crowd of shouting thousands pressed in upon us, carrying noisemakers and flaming torches.

Bishop Pedroza clung desperately to his saddle horn. In the light of the torches his face looked ghastly, not from fear, though he must have believed that danger was closing in on him from every side, but from some emotion deeper than physical fear, an assault upon his spirit. He must have seen many of the faithful moving down cathedral aisles in orderly processions. But never before had he looked into the countenance of a pagan multitude, nor felt its hot breath upon him, nor heard its wild, animal cries. Nothing in all Christendom had prepared him for this moment. Words formed on his lips but he could not speak them.

Guards made a path for us across the square to the gates of the temple and into its dark passageways. We rode in silence upward along gray walls dripping water, through nests of stalagmites that sprang from the earthen floor, past the Cavern of the Dead, where our torches shone upon endless rows of bleached skulls.

In all this journey, Bishop Pedroza said nothing. Only when

we came to the place where the skulls of those who had died on the sacrificial altar were carefully arranged, their white cheekbones touching in friendship, did a sound come from him, a gasp of horror, chilling to hear. But when we left our mounts behind and stepped out on the lofty terrace, Pedroza had regained his composure. Like someone just returned from a ride in the park, he glanced around indifferently, at the godhouse, at the stained stone altar, at the men in masks gathered beside it, and far below at the swarming multitude that filled the plaza.

Priests and lords were toiling up the steep face of the temple, zigzagging back and forth to lessen the strain on their legs. Among them, though he wore a mask, I made out the stooped figure of high priest Chalco, taking one deliberate step at a time, no doubt rehearsing the excuses he would offer for leaving us to die on the altar of the Aztéca war god.

At my side the dwarf, who was also watching, gave out his silly laugh, "He, he, he," and said, "It surprises me to see him here."

"The man never lacked for courage," I said.

"He has much to explain."

"We'll listen to his explanations. They'll be clever and believable. And we will accept them."

"In other words," said the dwarf, "we don't accept them. Now, before they are spoken, or later, when they are spoken."

"Neither now nor later," I said.

Votive candles lighted the terrace, shining on pools of half-dried blood left from a recent sacrifice. Bishop Pedroza must have seen the blood, but pretending, perhaps, that he stood on the well-swept stones of some Spanish cathedral, he did not take notice.

He stared down at the crowd that filled the square, at the Indians carrying torches streaming toward the temple from all directions, at the bobbing lights of canoes hurrying in from the sea. At last, as I moved forward to address the chanting crowd, he turned to me with dazed eyes in which I saw a look of bewilderment. Or was it apprehension I saw, or something stronger?

My speech to the multitude began with a few phrases of humble greeting. This was followed by an apology for my absence, reminding the people that I had returned to them after a journey much shorter than my first journey, when I had been gone a hundred years and more. I promised them that in times to come I would have more to say about my meeting with Moctezuma and with others.

Then I flung words at them like stones, like flaming javelins. "Your island and your city are in mortal danger," I said. "A barbarian, by name Hernán Cortés, came from a country far to the east. He landed upon the shores of Yucatán. With an army he marched to the city of the Aztéca, sacked the temples, and caused the death of Moctezuma. Finally he was driven from the city. But now he sulks. Now he gnashes his teeth. Now he cannot sleep, hatching plans to salve his wounded pride."

The chanting rose in waves and beat against the godhouse. Of the thousands in the square below, not one could hear me. But I was not talking to them. My words were meant for the lords gathered on the terrace, those who in my absence had listened to high priest Chalco, for the lesser priests who were in league with him, for Chalco himself. And above all, for the man in the black gown and violet vest, Bishop Rodrigo Pedroza.

"This Cortés," I went on, "this one who sulks and stews and licks his wounds, when he cannot sleep in the middle of the night, he nurses an idea. It is this. He plans to fall upon the Island of the Seven Serpents, upon us, and wreck our city as he did Tenochtitlán."

I waited until there was a lull in the chanting, then took a step forward to the very edge of the terrace and raised my hands. "I call you to arms," I shouted. In the silence that fell, I shouted it again. To those on the terrace, lowering my voice, I said, "All traitors, beware!" I said these words twice, so they could not be mistaken.

With this warning, I finished my speech. High priest Chalco then stepped forward to address the crowd. When he began an apology intended for me as well as for those in the square below, I gathered Bishop Pedroza, got him on his mare, and left the temple by the back passageway to avoid the crowd. We rode through the garden — where I was pleased to see flowers in bloom and fountains playing — to the palace.

I had planned to settle Pedroza in rooms next to those of Ah den Yaxche, who I thought would keep a watchful eye on the bishop, but to my great distress, the old man had died while I was gone. I had come to trust him and value his counsel. In the critical times ahead I would sorely miss him.

The quarters he had occupied were the most commodious in the palace, caught the morning sun like a golden net, and enjoyed an excellent view of the sacred lake where virgins were sacrificed to the sun god. Here I settled the bishop and ordered him a bountiful dinner, though he protested that he was not hungry.

"How long do you propose to keep me here?" he said as I was about to leave. "From your speech to the horde I gather that it will be some time."

"Some time indeed," I said. "The day Cortés is taken care of. Drowned in the sea or slain on the parapets."

Pedroza stood facing a wall that portrayed in blues and bright reds a scene from the terrace he had just left. It was inspired by the sacrifice of hundreds of slaves, whose bodies could be seen heaped in the background, their hearts piled high in a votive urn that was encircled by a serpent with amethyst eyes.

"In your speech," he said, "you warned that Cortés has already made plans to capture the city. If that is true, why do you prevent me from giving him the governor's message? It contains no secrets. Nothing that would help him in an attack upon you . . ."

The bishop paused, overcome, his eyes drawn to the mural in front of him. "Upon this barbaric island, whose inhabitants are the devil's savage spawn. Is it because you wish to hold me hostage?"

"Hostage?" I said. "The thought, I must confess, has never occurred to me. But it's a good one. If worse came to worst and Cortés was about to burn the city, Your Eminence might stay his hand rather than be burned yourself."

I waited for the bishop to answer, but his face had grown even paler and some emotion too strong for words kept him silent, his eyes fixed upon the wall.

• • • •

Two days before he died in his sleep, Ah den Yaxche had composed a message, which was delivered to me that night as I ate dinner. The hieroglyphics were painted on a scroll of the finest fawnskin paper, saved, no doubt, from the days when he was a high priest. There were only two glyphs in all, but the temple drum sounded the hour of midnight before I managed to make head or tail of them.

Ah den Yaxche, his blunt manner made more blunt by the shadow of death, and to the last refusing to address me as "god Kukulcán," had painted one of the parables in yellow and blue, showing a ruined cornfield, an empty hut, and a fat crow picking at an ear of corn. I interpreted it to mean that a farmer who leaves his land at harvest time will find upon returning that he has been robbed — a clear reference to my recent journey.

The second parable, limned starkly in yellows, reds, and blacks, showed a broad causeway branching into two paths, and a perplexed traveler standing at the fork, trying to decide which one to take. The path on his left was peopled by sleeping figures, happy beneath a bountiful tree, and beyond them low in the sky stood a warm, welcoming moon. The path on the traveler's right swarmed with fanged bats and eyeless snakes. But high in the heavens shone a gemlike star, bright as a ruby, whose rays touched the earth.

I puzzled over this parable into the night, slept upon it, awakened to it, then in the light of day put it out of mind.

The celebration that had started the previous night grew during the day. People came from distant parts of the island, from the mainland villages of Tikan, Zaya, Uxmat, and from the country of Mayapán. Wild cries and thundering drums beat against the palace walls like a summer *huracán.*

During this time Bishop Pedroza never left his room. Fearful after two days had passed that he had fallen ill, I went to his quarters and found him on his knees in prayer, his meals uneaten, the bed not slept in.

Seeing him there on his knees, hands clasped and pale face raised toward the sky, I was seized by a Christian impulse. Spanish blood joined us together. We were brothers in the faith. We both prayed to Mary, Mother of Christ. In Christ's name I should set him free.

The impulse lasted only an instant. It fled at the thought of Cortés and his army of brigands, who had sacked the city of Tenochtitlán, spreading fire and death among the innocent, who would do the same, if given the chance, in the City of the Seven Serpents. Quietly closing the door, I left the bishop on his knees.

The celebration lasted for more than a week and ended with the sacrifice of twenty-five slaves. I did nothing to stop the ritual, which pleased Chalco so much he made a special visit to the palace to thank me for my new attitude about the rite and to apologize for having deserted me in Tenochtitlán. I accepted both his thanks and his apologies with a nod.

"I hope you don't blame me for what happened there in the mountains," he said, speaking in a mousy voice through the open beak of his macaw mask, going on at length about his misfortunes.

"Why should I blame you?" I said. "You see me here, sitting in my favorite chair and in good health and spirits."

"You learned things from your journey to Moctezuma? You found him a bright and gentle man?"

"Gentle, but not bright. He lived by the stars, but the stars offered him bad counsel and in the end deserted him. You know that he's dead?"

"With sorrow I have heard," Chalco said, pausing to think. "The army that rides on the back of deer and carries thunder-sticks that spit fire, have you encountered it?"

I nodded.

"Do you believe that someday it will come here?"

"Someday." I knew, though I couldn't see the face behind the brilliant feathers of the macaw mask, that Chalco had given thought to this and was already laying plans, plans that would profit by Moctezuma's mistakes. "Someday soon," I added.

I had learned that after leaving Tenochtitlán and returning to the island, Chalco had spent his time courting the favor of the priesthood, which numbered close to nine hundred. By various deceits and promises of advancement, he had attracted a following of a dozen or more ambitious young priests. They felt that if I won the populace away from the Maya gods, they would find themselves with nothing to do, no ladders to climb.

The island and the city were threatened. All my strength, I felt, must go into meeting the onslaught of a barbarous army led by a brutal captain, whether they fell upon us in a month or a year. This was no time for a test of power between me and high priest Chalco and his ambitious cohorts. No time to waste on Christian thoughts. Christ was patient. He had waited for centuries. He would not mind waiting now, or so I concluded.

The dangerous journey to Tenochtitlán had been in vain. All I had learned about the nation that extended for a hundred leagues in every direction, about Moctezuma, its unstable king, to whom a thousand villages paid tribute, who with a single blast from a conch-shell horn could summon half a million warriors to his side — all this meant nothing. Everything I had seen — the fountains and running water, the lagoons blooming with hyacinth, the gardens along the streets and causeways and even on rooftops, the sky alive with feathered kites and flags — everything I remembered and hoped to bring to the City of the Seven Serpents now must be laid aside.

I ground my teeth in frustration and paced the palace floor. In anger, I then began the hateful task of turning a peaceful city into an armed camp.

I called the *nacom* to the palace and instructed him to begin fortifying the city at once. "In all directions," I said. "Strengthen the sea walls that have fallen. And devise a plan to protect us from attack by land."

"How much time to do all this?" the *nacom* said.

"Six months, no longer."

"But you told the man Pedroza that Cortés' army had been destroyed. In six months' time he cannot find a new army and march to the coast from the high mountains and get into ships and come here, not in six months."

"Cortés is an inventor of miracles," I said. "We may feel his hot breath sooner. In six months or less."

Under Flint Knife's watchful eye, repairs were started on the ruined walls between the city and the sea. In places they were little more than mounds of rubble overgrown by creeping vegetation. It was close to planting season, so I could not ask the farmers for help as I had before. Instead, the prisoners and slaves were set to work clearing the jungle and putting the stones back in place. With bitter disappointment I watched them leave the site at El Caracol and abandoned my plans of uncovering the series of mounds that lay beyond.

Heightening the harbor wall by two feet and lengthening it on both flanks called for more stones than were lying around. We sent masons to the ancient quarry, used hundreds of years before when the city was built, and cut slabs twice as large as those already in the walls. In the old days, stones had been hauled from the quarry to the building site on sleds. I hastened the operation by introducing the wheel, which for all of their brilliance the Maya had never thought of, or out of superstition never used. Or perhaps it was because some ruler had deemed it wise to give his restless subjects added work. In any event, carts on solid wooden wheels proved to be a vast improvement over sleds dragged by ropes.

The wall devoured stones, and while masons worked in the quarry we sent out carts and workmen to scrounge in the meadows around the palace, where huge buildings that once connected with it now lay in heaps. During this operation, which went on all day and by torches at night, Pedroza confronted me one evening as I sat down to dinner. I had not met the bishop since the day I left him on his knees, though I had seen him walking slowly through the meadow between the palace and the sacred lake, hands clasped behind his back.

I invited him to join me. He looked thinner than I remembered, and if possible, his face had a paler cast than usual.

"I have eaten," he said. "And now I would like to sleep. I have not done much of that lately, since the carts began rumbling all night."

"I'll have your quarters changed to the north wing of the palace," I said. "It will be quieter there, though you'll have no view of the lake."

"I'll stay it out," the bishop said, then paused, and a little color came into his face. He wore the large amethyst ring, which he began to twist. "However, since you are gathering stones for some reason, perhaps you could gather up the object that stands outside my window. Except for this unsightly pillar I would have an excellent view of the lake."

The object he referred to was really not a pillar at all, but a length of light green malachite, four times as tall as a tall man, carved in the shape of a male organ. Dozens of these fertility statues were scattered about the city.

The bishop backed toward the door. "I fail to see how you can countenance such an obscenity. And on the palace grounds."

"I'll have it taken down, carted away, and put in our wall," I said as he disappeared. "It will be gone by morning."

The wall progressed steadily until the day the bad news came. The road weasels I had sent to Tenochtitlán returned with word that Cortés was busy collecting the remnants of his army and, far from admitting defeat, planned another attack upon the Aztéca.

The news spurred us to greater effort. Working hours were increased. Fires were built and men toiled in shifts. Silversmiths laid down their tools, fishermen put aside their nets, farmers deserted the fields, everyone joined in to finish the wall that would hold off the army of Hernán Cortés.

In the midst of all this feverish toil came the rites of spring. I wished to delay them for a week, but at a meeting of the Council of Elders the three old men questioned the wisdom of such a delay. The rites were centuries old, they said; the magic chain should not be broken, lest the gods be outraged and vent their wrath upon the city. I would have won out, however, had it not been for high priest Chalco.

In a black robe, a jaguar mask with catlike eyes and terrifying fangs that covered his sensitive face, he strode back and forth in front of the throne, jerking his short arms, stopping to stare at me from time to time, speaking in a feline voice not his own.

"The city cowers," he said. "It quakes. It trembles. All because this white man appeared mysteriously out of the east, saying that he was sent by a powerful god and king to rule over all the Indian lands, the Aztéca, the Toltéca, the Maya, over this city, over everyone. This white man . . ." Here Chalco paused to let these last words settle in the minds of the three elders. "This white man," he repeated, "that Moctezuma to his sorrow mistook for the god Quetzalcoatl, known to us as Kukulcán . . ." Again Chalco paused. My name hung in the air. ". . . This white man was driven from the streets of Tenochtitlán by the brown Aztéca, humiliated and his army slain. Yet our proud city trembles at the word *Cortés*. And out of fear cannot stop work long enough to greet Xipe Totec and the coming of spring. Shame upon us!"

Two young priests standing to one side of him said, "Shame," in quiet voices. The three old men whispered to each other. The dwarf crouching at my side said, *"Cuidado."* I was silent.

A gentle rain was falling, but through the windows I caught a glimpse of Bishop Pedroza walking bareheaded in the meadow. I saw him stoop to pluck a flower, then cast a prayerful look toward the heavens.

Chalco, following my gaze, said, "We worry about a white man, without an army, far off in Tenochtitlán. But here among us —" He pointed to the meadow. The three elders turned to look. "— we have a white man who has been heard to laugh at our dress. At the way we conduct ourselves. And worse, who scoffs at our gods!"

An elder said, "The rites of spring will be celebrated. Is it possible to rid ourselves of the one who walks in the rain without a cloak, who picks flowers, and who scoffs at the gods?"

"It is possible," said Chalco.

I rose to my feet. "It is not possible," I said quietly, aware, should Pedroza die, that I would lose my chance of taking the orders of priesthood. "If this man who walks in the rain without a cloak is so much as touched, I will see that the one who does the touching pays for it with his life."

A sweep of my hand dismissed the assemblage.

"God forgive me," I said, "but I wish this Chalco had breathed his last. Will no one rid me of this upstart priest?"

"Sometimes I too have this wish," the dwarf said. "I have had the wish for some time. He, he, he."

The dwarf spoke in his usual jocular way, yet beneath the simpering words I detected a note that I had never heard before.

While work on the great stone wall went on day and night, the damaged caravel, which we had towed back from the bay of Ixtlilzochitl, was not neglected. New masts were made. Women set up looms in the square, as they had before, where all could admire their work, and wove new sails, using the best of cotton, blending into them the insignia of Kukulcán, Lord of the Evening Star, a red ball surrounded by a sunburst of golden rays.

Delfín Azul was not a fitting name for a Maya caravel, but since it brings ill fortune to change the name of a ship, *Delfín Azul* she remained, with a blue dolphin as a figurehead.

I was in dire need of workers. The corn from last year's harvest was running low. Chalco's *tecuítcal* — the nourishing green moss he had brought from Tenochtitlán — had flourished, but there wasn't enough of it yet to feed the city. To meet the problem of impending hunger I was forced to send the fishermen — some sixty of them — back to sea.

The *nacom* suggested that since I had drained all the men from Zaya, Uxmat, and Tikan, I might visit a town he had heard of called Chichén-Palapa, three days' sail to the south.

I decided to make the journey, not only to gather workers to replace the fishermen, but also to try out the *Delfín Azul,* her cannon, and her crew. The night before my departure I sent for Bishop Pedroza, thinking that I might lighten his days by giving him something to do besides walk in the meadow glued to his breviary.

He came to the dining room as I was finishing my evening meal. Although he knew the custom, observed by everyone else, of appearing barefoot, eyes downcast, touching the floor with the brow, he walked in stiffly as he had before, his heavy boots creaking, squinting at me out of his cold gray eyes.

I had not seen him in weeks, except for fleeting glimpses as he strolled about in the meadow. He looked even paler than he had before.

"Your Eminence," I said, letting him stand, "I leave tomorrow for Chichén-Palapa. It's a town some hundred leagues to the south. I go there to enlist the aid of its ruler, Matlazingo, against any attack that Cortés might launch against my island."

Pedroza glanced about the vast room and after a while casually in my direction. I could tell that he wanted to know how Hernán Cortés was faring, but would rather be put in chains than ask.

"Cortés," I said, "has pulled parts of his beaten army together and collected his Indian allies. From reports I received two days ago, he has blocked the roads that lead into Tenochtitlán and has placed the city under siege."

Bishop Pedroza betrayed no emotion at this news.

"The Aztéca nation is divided, its leaders fighting among themselves, killing each other," I said. "Cortés will take advantage of this. He'll starve the city into submission before the year is out."

The bishop stirred himself. "Since you believe this," he said, "would it not be better for me to go on to Tenochtitlán and deliver the governor's message and speak a word in your behalf? Then in the spring, when, as you say, Cortés knocks at your door, he will look more kindly upon you and the island."

"In the first place, Bishop, I doubt that you would say one

single word in my behalf. Second, knowing Hernán Cortés, I am certain that if you did, he would not listen. Hernán is not a listener."

Servants brought in a steaming jug of coca leaf tea and I offered the bishop a cup, which he refused.

"You must have some mission," I said, "more important than delivering a message from the Governor of Hispaniola. This could be done by a page boy."

"The message is important," Pedroza said. "After it has been delivered, I will turn my attention elsewhere. To the thousands who are in grave danger of losing their immortal souls. Your savages have a great attachment to their heathen gods. I marvel at it. I wish that many Christians possessed half their zeal. It should not be impossible, therefore, to give their zeal a different direction."

"Not impossible, sir, but difficult. I brought you here to tell you what I have done. It is this. Every morning I appear in the plaza and greet the rising sun with a few of Christ's words. I speak in Latin and Spanish and Maya. But it doesn't matter what language I speak. It's the sound of the voice rather than the words that holds the Indians. And in Maya, Christian words have little meaning. They never translate well."

The temple drum boomed out the hour. Its echoes faded into the drumming of the rain. Pedroza stood stiffly erect, looking down at me, a sudden, suspicious glint in his gaze.

"Do you speak Maya?" I said. "I know that you understand it. You were following my conversation with the *nacom*."

"I understand more than I speak," Pedroza said. "I studied Maya as well as Aztéca in Hispaniola. The church has a class in Indian dialects. Maya is a strange language. It rolls around on the epiglottis like a mouthful of square pebbles. It reminds me . . ."

"When I leave tomorrow," I said, "you will take over my religious duties. I'll introduce you to the people at dawn. There'll be a thousand of them, at least. Don't overburden them with talk. And don't be surprised when, as dawn breaks, they prick their fingers with thorns, then hold the bright blood up to the rising sun."

Pedroza twisted his ring, the only sign that he had been taken by surprise.

"In the years I have been here, Bishop Pedroza, I haven't conducted mass or heard confessions or given hope to those who were dying. I couldn't, for as you know, I am not a priest."

"I understand. Yes, a seminarian. It was wise of you not to conduct yourself like a priest. To assume powers that did not belong to you."

His voice was churchly, soft and understanding, but beneath it lay a hard little thread of disapproval. Candlelight winked on his violet ring, spread a luminous sheen upon his fine violet vest. For a fleeting moment, as once before, I was shaken by envy.

"More could have been done, Your Eminence, had I been blessed with priestly power. There has been a hollow place where my heart should be. It has haunted me. It still does."

"It should," Pedroza said, but not unkindly. "There's the beginning of a seminary in Hispaniola. Five students. How many years of study do you lack?"

"One. Less than one."

"I suggest that you go there and resume your studies. I will give you a letter to the governor, which will go a long way toward absolving you of the . . . from the crimes committed here."

It was on my tongue to shout an angry reply. But I waited for several moments, listening to the rain and the far-off thunder, cooling my tongue.

"It occurs to me," I said, in the most logical tone I could summon, "that by the simple laying of your hands upon my head, you can ordain me a priest."

Pedroza took a step back. He muttered something in Latin — an appeal to God, I believe.

"My vocation has been approved by Archbishop Sosa in Seville," I said. "There are only a few months of study left to me. What I would learn in that time is not half of what I would learn here among the Indians. Not one hundredth of what I have already learned."

"Learned as a pagan king?"

"Learned," I said.

Bishop Pedroza was retreating toward the door. He stopped and stood a moment in silence. "Give up this heathenish business," he said. "Cleanse your soul by saying a thousand Hail Marys. During the night I will think of other, more severe penances. Go to Hispaniola and resume your studies. I will see that you are ordained. That I promise."

I did not seek an answer. "Keep your penances," I said. "You may need them yourself."

Bishop Pedroza did not appear in the plaza at dawn.

While people cheered from the new embankment, drums beat, and trumpets screeched, the *Delfín Azul* sailed out on a fresh wind, splendid under her new sails.

The *Santa Margarita* remained at the wharf, since she held the vast treasure from Isla del Oro and the priceless Aztéca hoard the dwarf had collected in Tenochtitlán. He had placed a heavy guard upon her and moved aboard himself to keep an eye on the ship, now that there were those in the city who had learned the value of gold.

After a brief tilt with a storm that ripped our foresail, we arrived at the port of Chichén-Palapa late in the afternoon of the third day.

The village — reported by the *nacom* to be a town — lay inland at the head of a deep-water lagoon lined with palms. As we approached it shots from the falconets announced our arrival. A fleet of canoes came leisurely from some hidden place, carrying warriors in black paint and red macaw plumes.

Their leader was a spindly little man in a huge monkey mask that had a monkey's long tail dangling out behind it. I shouted down to him to come aboard. He thought for a while, then pointed in the direction of a beach where the rest of Chichén-Palapa was beginning to gather.

I had a well-armed crew row me ashore, and there on the sand, with a crowd around us and pink crabs scuttling underfoot, the cacique and I warily faced each other and began to talk, one slow Maya word at a time.

He had never heard of the Island of the Seven Serpents, and since he took me at once for a Spaniard, I made no mention of being Kukulcán, Lord of the Winds, God of the Painted Arrows. Gerónimo de Aguilar he had seen and talked to soon after the shipwrecked Spaniard had become the cacique of a neighboring village.

"Aguilar is a good man," the cacique said. "Therefore you are a good man, too. All men in that country over there you call Spain are good men."

"Not all," I said. "There's a man you may encounter sometime who is not good. He has red hair and a red beard and white skin like a dead man. If you do something he does not like, he will cut your foot off. Or your hand. Or perhaps your head."

"He is from Spain? No."

"From Spain. He is called Hernán Cortés."

The cacique made a chattering sound between his teeth, a sign of disbelief, and though I described the massacre at Chólolan, with blood running in the streets and parts of people lying around, nothing I said about Cortés changed his mind. He still made the little monkeylike sounds.

When I had finished with Cortés, he took off his mask and opened his mouth and drew forth a small wad of something he had been chewing on, which looked much like a cow's cud. He spat it out on the sand and at once a servant darted forth and gave him a handful of dried, gray-green leaves. The servant then gave some of the leaves to me.

"Coca," the chief said.

He stuffed the leaves into his mouth until his cheeks bulged, and I did the same with mine. After he had chewed for a while he said, "Good."

I nodded. It was similar to the leaf brewed into the tea that I drank, only much stronger.

I now noticed that everyone around us had bulging cheeks. And everyone, like the cacique himself, appeared to be happy. Except for the narcotic leaves they were chewing, there didn't seem to be any reason for happiness. All were barefooted and clad in rags, including the cacique.

Through the trees I could see a row of ruined buildings scattered along both banks of a river. A mound with a cotton tree growing boldly from its top could once have been a temple. Beyond it, an edifice much like El Caracol stood nearly submerged in a sea of vegetation, wild green waves lapping against it. On the far side of the river were stretches of tumbled walls, like my own before I began the task of rebuilding.

"The city of Chichén-Palapa is fast disappearing," I said. "In another year it will be gone."

The cacique wrinkled his wizened little face and smiled sadly. He looked as much like a monkey as he did when he was wearing the mask.

"Sooner, perhaps," he said, still smiling.

"How many workers do you count?" I asked.

"One thousand. Almost half are farmers. Half fish for pearls. The others are traders. They sell the pearls."

"Where? We buy pearls, but your traders never come to my island. Why?"

"No, we go to the south with our pearls," he said, but pointing to the north, "to the land of the Inca. That is where they grow the fine coca. You like this coca? Good."

The river was wide and ran past the temple toward far-distant hills. I asked the cacique if there was another city on its banks — using the word *city* because it seemed to please him to think of Chichén-Palapa as a city.

"Many," he said. "Two."

"Big?"

"Not so big as Chichén-Palapa."

"You trade?"

"They bring corn and we trade."

"Corn for coca?"

"All the time, but this year trading was bad. They have a war down there in the Inca country, so the coca is scarce, so they mix the coca leaves with leaves that look like coca, ceiba leaves maybe, and then they mix everything up with lots of lime. You taste the lime? Too much?"

"Too much," I said and took this as an excuse to remove my cud and quietly bury it in the sand.

"Next year," the cacique said, losing his smile, "when my traders go to the Inca country, they will take pearls that have little cracks deep down that you cannot see unless you know about them."

As my stomach ceased to turn and I picked the last of the leaves from my teeth, I began to wonder if the decline of the Maya nation was not due to the use of this coca drug. What had happened in Chichén-Palapa could be an example of what had happened elsewhere, over the centuries. If not the whole cause, it could well have been the principal one.

I had come to the village with the hope of taking back a shipload of Indians, but the Chichén-Palapas were such a miserable lot that I now gave up the idea in disgust. Night was drawing near. I bade the cacique goodbye.

"Come back, Spaniard," he said. "Spaniards are always welcome in my kingdom."

"Not the man with the red hair and the ghostlike face," I warned the cacique. "If you see him, run fast and hide in the hills."

The cacique shed tears as I climbed into the longboat and conches sounded a sad farewell. When I reached the caravel I had one of the lombards fired in reply. While we were headed into the open sea, navigator Tunac-Eel tattooed his broad chest with a small notation about the port, beside other notes he had accumulated over the years, though I promised him that we would never return to Chichén-Palapa.

He set our course by the North Star, and with fair weather we arrived home just seven days after we had left. In that time my people had quit work and crowded into the temple square to watch Xipe Totec, god of spring, in the person of one of the young priests, dance from dawn to dusk attired in the flayed skin of a slave.

After he had danced for three days, the rites of spring came to an end with a ceremony at Chac Balam.

It was held every seventh year — the number seven had a special magic for the priesthood — on a night of a full moon. Late in the day, after Xipe Totec had ended his dance, the city gathered on the shores of the sacred lake.

Broad meadows formed three sides of Chac Balam, but on the fourth side, which faced the rising moon, there was a high, sheer cliff and at its crest a shelf of rock that served as an altar.

Until night came, tumult reigned in the meadows. Clowns painted in riotous hues of yellow and red tumbled about on the grass. Boys on stilts waded along the shore. Kites flew overhead, though none so beautiful as those I had seen in the Aztéca skies. And adding to the tumult was an uproar of drums, trumpets, whistles, rattles, and thousands of voices wild with excitement.

At dusk priests lit copal fires, seven on each side of the altar and seven at the back. Silence fell across the meadow. Far off in the city, dogs began to bark.

I stood behind the altar, unnoticed under a ceiba tree, the dwarf at my side. I had no part in the ceremony. I was only there because my absence at the most important of all the Maya rites could not have been explained. In white-thonged sandals, white gown, and a serpent mask, Chalco stood in front of me. A row of his black-gowned priests surrounded him, holding in their arms spring flowers and ahuehuetl branches.

The dark horizon paled. Conch horns began to moan along

the shore and a chorus of voices joined them, rising and falling in a whispered chant to Ix Chel, Goddess of the Moon, Goddess of Love on Earth. A star, her herald and outrider, appeared low in the east. The chanting ceased. In the deep silence the goddess appeared at the door of night, robed in gold.

There was the sound of voices on the far side of the ceiba tree, followed by a muffled protest and footsteps among dry leaves. A girl dressed in white slipped past me, past high priest Chalco, to the front of the altar. She had black hair that fell to her waist and a garland of flowers on her brow. I could not see her face, but from her lithe figure and youthful movements, I judged her to be no more than twelve.

She stood there on the narrow ledge, clasping her hands as if she were not quite certain what was expected of her. She turned her head, seeking counsel, and I caught a glimpse of her face. It was the face of a child, a frightened child who was trying to be brave.

Chalco glided forward and took her hand. He said something to her under his breath and with his fingers gave her a gentle little push. She now clasped her hands upon her breast and took a halting step toward the ledge. She glanced down into the black waters of Chac Balam and drew back.

A murmur rose from the meadow, a vast sigh of adoration. I am not certain that I heard Chalco say, "Ix Chel looks down upon you."

The full moon shone upon us. Fires were burning on both sides of the altar. Yet I am not certain of what next took place. The dwarf ran past me, this I know. I saw him hold up his hands. I saw the child move forward and without a word, her white dress gathered about her, the garland of flowers still binding her hair, leap out into the night.

There was a moment of awful silence. The sound of the waters parting and the faintest of cries. Then I saw that the dwarf had run forward, seemingly in an effort to reach the child, and had somehow become entangled with Chalco. Or, in an attempt to stop the dwarf, had Chalco reached out and grasped him as he ran past?

It did not matter. I rushed out to separate the struggling men. Before I reached them, Chalco had managed to free himself. As he did so, he took a step backward, stumbled, and vainly trying to catch himself, tumbled headlong over the cliff, screaming as he went.

Riding homeward in a litter borne by six quiet retainers, through a stunned crowd, I said little to the dwarf and that about nothing. Not until we were in the throne room, with the servants sent away and the doors bolted, did I ask him to explain what had happened at Chac Balam.

"He, he, he," the dwarf laughed, doing a few steps of the *jota*. "High priest Chalco fell off a high cliff and got himself drowned."

"Chalco's death is not something for laughter," I said.

"You wish me to cry?" the dwarf asked. "Since you're not shedding tears, I'll be glad, if you wish, to shed them for you."

"What took place? Whose fault was it? Chalco's?"

The dwarf started to laugh again, pointed a toe for a *jota* step, then straightened himself as he met my eye.

"I am surprised that you should ask," he said. "I guess you've forgotten that not long ago — it was the day you had the argument with the high priest — you said, and I repeat your words, 'God forgive me, will no one rid me of this upstart priest?' "

"Words shouted in anger."

"You may remember that King Henry of England, speaking of Thomas à Becket, also shouted in anger so loud that all could hear, 'What cowards have I about me that no one will deliver me from this lowborn priest?' "

"What has King Henry to do with me?"

"Well, there were men around the king who were not cowards. Four of them. And they stabbed Becket as he knelt in prayer."

It took me a moment to gather my wits. "You mean that you weren't trying to save the child?"

"No, she had leaped already."

"You meant to kill Chalco?"

"You saw what happened. Did it look like murder?"

"It happened too fast. I don't know what I saw."

"You saw Chalco grab my thin little arm. Give my poor body a horrible twist."

"I saw the two of you struggling on the cliff's edge."

"A frightful moment. I thought I was a goner."

"You may be a goner yet. Chalco's cohorts won't take his death lightly."

The dwarf frowned. "How do *you* take his death? Does it disturb you as Becket's death disturbed the king? Truthfully."

"Truthfully, less. It's the child's death that disturbs me."

"She was too young to die," the dwarf said. "And so is Guillermo Cantú. For a few days, until this event blows over, it may be wise for him to disappear. Take up residence on the *Santa Margarita*."

The dwarf wouldn't stay for dinner, but hurried off, and when it was served I turned my back on it and got down on my knees in prayer.

The child's death obsessed me. I had watched hundreds die on the stone altar, their hearts lifted out and dropped in the votive jars or thrown to the waiting throng. The scenes had sickened me, more at first than of late, yet all of them together had not been nearly so disturbing as the death of this one child. What was her name? What mother would mourn her loss? What friends? Or would she be mourned at all?

She looked to be the same age as my sister, no older than nine. Yet it was not my sister I thought of while I prayed.

Nor the sight of the child plunging to her death. It was the cry that escaped her lips when the dark waters gathered her in that haunted me, a cry which was little more than a whisper, not of fear but of regret at leaving a life she had never lived.

At dawn I was borne out to the square to face a crowd much larger than I had seen for weeks, drawn there by Chalco's death. Afterward I went to the harbor to talk with Cantú.

He was in the hold, making a tally of the treasure he had accumulated in the past two years — the gold from Isla del Oro, the gold that quietly, unbeknownst to me, he had stripped from the walls and sarcophagus of the king's tomb, and the gold bars Cortés had divided among his men on the night he fled from Tenochtitlán. A mammoth hoard — more than twenty-three tons, by the dwarf's careful computations — so heavy that while it would serve as good ballast in a storm, it burdened the *Santa Margarita* so much that she now had little space between her decks and the water.

"There's a lot more in El Caracol," the dwarf complained. "Five tons alone, in the door to the king's chamber. More inside . . ."

"Leave it," I said. "The ship has scarcely enough freeboard as things stand. She'll be a slow sailer even in a gale. In fair winds, she'll sit still. It might be wise to lighten her. Put some of the weight on the *Delfín*."

"I don't trust her crew. When I came aboard last night one of them greeted me. A sharp-eyed little Indian I had ordered off the *Santa Margarita* once before. He wanted to know where all the gold had come from. I ordered him off the ship again and told him not to come back. I don't trust any of them over there on the *Delfín.*"

"This ship will make a marvelous fort," I said, "but not a fighting ship. We can station the fort out in the harbor, around the first of the channel markers. Move all of her cannon to port. Anchor her forward and aft, broadside to the direction that Cortés must appear from. In other words, we will block the channel."

"He, he, he," said the dwarf. "*Excelente!* When will we do all this? Tomorrow?"

"Today. The crowd this morning was buzzing about Chalco's death. I heard your name spoken. We'll move the ship. Get her away from the wharf and any of the crowd that might take a notion to come here wanting to talk."

"When do you look for Cortés?" the dwarf asked. "The road weasel that came in last week said he had recaptured Tenochtitlán."

"Word yesterday was that this happened a month ago. What's important is that while he laid siege to Tenochtitlán, Cortés was also building ships at Vera Cruz. They are ready to sail. In the meantime, he's sent Alvarado — you'll remember him as the captain who was always about to choke Moctezuma — started him south with a small army. Cortés himself is on his way to Vera Cruz. He could sail any time."

"With how many ships?"

"The spies don't know."

"He might sail in here any day."

"It's possible."

The dwarf grew serious. "Can the bishop be of help to us? Cortés, you'll remember, is very religious. A bishop, especially one with a message from the Governor of Hispaniola, should carry weight with him. That is, if worst comes to worst." The dwarf paused to cross himself. "And we are forced to sue for peace."

"I have already talked to him about this, but he will not help us. I am on my way now to have another talk with the bishop. On a different matter."

I found Pedroza in his room, looking out at the meadow where the grass was turning green and larks were flying. From his window he had a fine view of the lake and the cliff above. He must have watched the procession wind past on its way to Chac Balam, heard the tumult as the people celebrated the coming of spring, the hush as they watched for the moon to rise, seen fires burning on the cliff and the child waiting in her white gown and garland of flowers to offer herself to Yum Kaax, the god of corn.

"You were there to watch," the bishop said. "To participate."

"Only to watch," I said.

"To watch and not to raise your voice against it is to participate. Being there, your very presence condoned this . . . this" — Pedroza had difficulty with the word — "this barbarous rite."

"The rite is very old," I said. "Hieroglyphics show that it took place before Christ was born. That long ago. Do you think I have the power to end something that ancient? How is this done? By decree?"

"Cortés managed it with the Aztéca. I have seen his letters."

"By slaying the Aztéca. By destroying their temples."

"And using the stones to build Christian churches."

Pedroza had grown a beard since I saw him last. Black and flowing, it gave him a powerful, untamed look that could have belonged to God in one of His angrier moods.

"From the sea at Vera Cruz," I said, "to the mountains of Tenochtitlán, Cortés cut a bloody path, maiming and killing and destroying. He will do the same here if he gets the chance."

"Cortés," the bishop said, "is conquering pagan lands for the king and the glory of Christ. While you cheat the king and mock Christ. Yesterday I went to the square at dawn. I stood in the crowd and heard you sing the Salve Regina and speak of the Redeemer. Then, in the next breath, you were a pagan lord thrusting a bloody finger toward the sun, like the thousands that pressed about you."

"A token, Your Eminence."

"In the kingdom of Christ, there are no tokens." The bishop shook his fist. " 'Thou shalt have no other gods before me. Thou shalt not make unto thee any graven image or likeness of any thing that is in heaven above or that is in the earth below or that is in the water under the earth.' "

His thundering words echoed in the room. He turned away and came back.

"Go to the temple," he said in a gentle voice. "Go and stand on the terrace before the godhouse, surrounded by the shades of the thousands who were slain there, and announce to all that you are a humble Spaniard and not the Lord Kukulcán."

"Who would believe me?" I asked, trying to picture myself on the terrace, blurting out such a confession. "Who?"

"You yourself would believe," Pedroza said. "This belief and the confession of guilt is what matters. They are the first steps you must take to save your soul from the eternal fires of hell."

I was growing impatient. I hadn't come here to be lectured. "When I arrived in the City of the Seven Serpents," I said, "the streets were clogged with fallen stones. People wandered through them lamenting the days of Kukulcán. They had never heard Christ's name spoken. Now they have. I was rebuilding the city when Cortés appeared among the Aztéca. I was spreading Christ's message as best I could. Now, when the people are in peril, you ask me to desert them."

"Your soul is more important than a city inhabited by savages," Bishop Pedroza said.

The big drum boomed in the temple, announcing midday.

It shook the room, scattered the birds in the meadow, and caused the bishop to put his hands over his ears.

"A heathenish sound," he said. "But when Cortés captures the city we shall hear the celestial voice of bells. They will come from the best foundries in Spain."

"Cortés will not capture my city, Your Eminence. If he tries, he will be killed."

The bishop glanced at me to make sure that I was in earnest. "I see that besides your other sins you have turned against Spain, your own country."

"Not against Spain," I said, "only against those she sends here. Like Cortés and his lieutenants."

"These brave men may find their graves in the land of the Aztéca," the bishop said. "But in Spain thousands are anxious to take their place. In Hispaniola hundreds crowd the harbor waiting for ships. Draw back from the abyss, Julián Escobar, before it is too late . . ."

The sound of chanting interrupted his lecture. A line of priests wound slowly up the path that led from Chac Balam to the Temple of Kukulcán. The last six were supporting a litter, on which rested the remains of high priest Chalco. In their black gowns that were stiff with blood, with their long, unwashed hair hanging like hanks of rusty metal halfway down their backs, they looked like a procession of carrion birds.

The bishop held his nose, as if he smelled a carrion odor. His amethyst ring caught the sun. His gown and violet colored vest were clean. How different he appeared against the procession of Maya priests, how civilized and elegant!

Behind Pedroza was the power of the Holy Roman Empire, the Church, the king, the Council of the Indies, the powerful Governor of Hispaniola, the long line of tradition, of civilization itself. And here was I, a seminarian masquerading as a god, the ruler of a half-ruined city inhabited by pagan Indians who, after months of exhortation and Christian love, still worshipped the sun and sacrificed girl children to celebrate the planting of corn and the coming of spring.

"Your Eminence," I said as the chanting faded in the distance and the room grew quiet, "I have spoken to you before about this matter. Our conversation was brief and unsatisfactory. I asked you to honor me by bestowing upon me a priesthood. You refused to do so, giving me instead some undigested advice and a long list of penances."

Pedroza began to worry his violet ring, slowly turning it round and round on his finger.

"I am making the request again, sir. This time I expect you to grant it. Cortés or one of his numerous captains, all of them scoundrels, are making a sweep southward along the coast. They will arrive here any day, any hour. You are aware that we will defend ourselves. And that it will be a time of turmoil. My people will be injured. Some may die. I wish to have the power of administering absolution and last rites."

Pedroza gave a polite snort. "How can you absolve someone who has no soul? A savage? Or say last rites over a soulless creature?"

"There are ways," I said, "and I will find them."

"Not as a priest," the bishop said, "for I refuse your request. Now, today, and tomorrow. Take heed. Hernán Cortés is an emissary of the Church and the king. Do not oppose him."

"He comes searching for gold. To find it he'll ransack the temples, turn the city upside down, and slay anyone who threatens or resists him."

"Welcome Cortés with flowers and song, and I will see that he does no harm to the people."

"With songs and flowers Moctezuma welcomed him into the city of the Aztéca. And Cortés burned the temples and slew the people."

On the table beside his bed was Pedroza's Bible. I picked

it up. "There are verses I want to read, Your Eminence. Things I have forgotten. Tomorrow we'll meet for further discussion."

The bishop frowned, not pleased that I had his Bible.

"There is nothing to discuss," he said. "Give up this play-acting. Welcome Cortés to the city. Go to Hispaniola and again take up your studies. Only then will I discuss the matter with you."

"We'll discuss it tomorrow," I said and closed the door softly behind me.

• • •

The Council of Elders came to see me shortly after the priests went by with Chalco's body. The old men wished to declare the full week of mourning demanded by the death of someone of importance. I tried to convince them that the city was in hourly danger, that it could ill afford to spend that much time in lamentations.

Two of our most reliable weasels arrived while this argument was taking place. They came separately and with different stories. One reported that an attempt had been made on Cortés' life, led by a soldier named Villafaña. The plot was discovered and the culprit had tried to swallow his list of conspirators — among them prominent men in Spain and Hispaniola — but failed and was hung at once from his window ledge.

This report placed Cortés in Tenochtitlán, at least a month away, but the second weasel brought word that a Spanish fleet had been sighted at Ixtlilzochitl, the port where we had found the *Delfín Azul.* This information, fortunately, backed me up and we compromised on three days of mourning.

Since the people had already enjoyed a full week of ceremonies, I was reluctant to give them more time to indulge themselves. They were devout believers in an earthly heaven, where you worked when you had to and spent the rest of your hours either mourning or rejoicing, so long as it was the will of friendly gods. In the old days, when the magnificent city was conceived and built, they must have had a different attitude about work.

Chalco's cohorts, those who had taken his body from Chac Balam, already were going about the streets dressed in skeleton masks, making prophecies of disaster. Crops would fail. Plagues would rain down. St. John the Baptist would erupt and bury the city in ashes. Before the day was out I rounded them up — fifty-nine in all — and sent them by ship to the southern part of the island, to a village of farmers who worshipped at a ruined temple. They were given tools and told to clear away the jungle and replace the fallen stones. The task would remove them from the city at a time of impending peril and keep them busy for a year at least.

On the two journeys Chalco had made to Tenochtitlán, he had brought back nearly a hundred Aztéca porters. I had always believed that they were not porters but assassins in disguise and that he planned to use them against me. My suspicions were quickly borne out, for that very night, fearing for their lives, no doubt, they stole three of our big sailing canoes and disappeared.

I was glad to see the last of them, though I could ill afford to lose the big canoes.

Further news came after I had eaten dinner and was reading the Bible I had taken from Pedroza.

The Spanish fleet, made up of two large caravels and a small pinnace, had left the bay at Ixtlilzochitl. It was heading south, the weasel thought, but because of a *chubasco* he was not sure of the direction. (I had borrowed Moctezuma's system of fast runners — *andadores,* I called them — who ran two leagues and passed their messages to a second runner. And so forth, night and day, to a village across the strait, whence they were brought to the island by canoe.)

At midnight I received news that the Spanish fleet was

headed south in our direction. It sent me and the *nacom* out to inspect our defenses. The wall now completely enclosed the harbor on three sides. The *Delfín Azul* lay at the end of the channel. We had removed half her cannon and mounted them on each arm of the bay, three to each side. The dwarf had taken the *Santa Margarita* to the channel entrance and anchored her broadside to the sea, as I had planned.

The warriors who had fought at Tikan were in readiness behind the wall, armed with spears, copper-headed arrows, and muskets. The *Santa Margarita* was too heavily laden with gold, the crew of the *Delfín Azul* too inexperienced, for either of the ships to venture out and fight at sea. But they were in position to repel an attack. Furthermore, any landings the Spaniards might make along the coast would fail because the few trails that led into the city wound through heavy, easily defended jungle.

My one great problem was with the populace itself. No one was in a mood to fight, or even to listen to the rumors of a possible fight. They had never seen the cold gray eyes of Hernán Cortés, nor his army of marauding Spaniards dressed in steel, mounted on horses protected by steel, carrying weapons that spat death from a distance, bearded men asking no quarter and giving none. My efforts to rally them were futile.

Their chief concern when the *nacom* and I made a tour of the fortifications and talked to the crews of both ships was the search for a dog, a yellow dog, which was needed for Chalco's funeral. A man of his standing could not be buried unless he was accompanied by a small yellow dog who would see him safely across the river and into the other world. There were many small dogs in the city, but none was yellow. Priests solved the problem late that afternoon by painting a small white dog with yellow ocher.

Thereafter, preparations for the burial went forward. Green

boughs and flowers were gathered and seven slaves whom Chalco had marked for sacrifice on a coming feast day were anointed with oil and given fresh gowns to wear.

The Council of Elders met and suggested by messenger that I appoint in Chalco's position an elderly priest, Tecoa Pital, whom Chalco had managed to defeat in the contest for high priest the year I came to the island. I lost no time in accepting this soft-spoken man. They also suggested that they would like to talk with the dwarf and asked if I would send word for him to appear before them the following day.

Knowing that all the king's fine horses could never drag Cantú away from the *Santa Margarita,* still I sent messages to the ship, one written in Maya, asking him to come at once, and one written in Spanish, warning him not to come, not until the rumors concerning Chalco's death had had a chance to die after the battle that was rapidly taking shape.

And the rumors would die after the battle, for whichever way it went, the City of the Seven Serpents would never again be the same. The city would be either an armed camp, always on the alert to fend off attacks from other adventurers, or a city ruled by Spaniards, without even a memory of a Council of Elders, a thousand priests, and the god Kukulcán, Lord of the Evening Star.

The *chubasco* at Ixtlilzochitl swept down the coast and fell upon us at dusk, battering the city with heavy winds and torrents of rain. Further news of the Spanish fleet could not be expected until the storm blew itself out, which would not occur for two days at least.

Thinking to put Bishop Pedroza in a mood to hear what I had to say, I sent him an invitation to join me for dinner. When after a long wait his refusal came back, I ordered guards to bring him to the throne room.

I greeted him from the throne with a curt nod and let him stand in his neat cassock and violet-colored vest, his high forehead white with anger.

"There was little chance today to more than glance at the Bible," I said, "but a thought about what I did read comes to mind. The Bible says that God loves all men, of whatever color, those with souls and those without souls, equally. Your ideas about the Indians are different from God's. That may explain why you are such a keen admirer of Hernán Cortés and the cruel means he uses to subdue them."

I waited for the bishop to answer, but he stood disdainfully stiff and silent.

"Unlike Cortés and you, Your Eminence, I believe that the Indians on this island are God's creatures and I have treated them as such. My work has suffered because I lack the authority to convert them to the Christian faith."

"We have gone over this before," Pedroza broke in. "I readily admit that you have the training for the priesthood, but for the last time, I advise you to declare the gold you have collected and to give up your heathenish masquerade. If you do, I will help to further your vocation. If you do not, then I'll denounce you to the king, the Governor of Hispaniola, and to Cortés."

"Who will be here soon," I said. "Unless he drowns in the storm."

A gust of wind found its way through a crack in the roof and lifted the bishop's gown, revealing his stout, white legs. Unruffled, he settled himself and started for the door.

"A moment." I got to my feet. "Chalco, the high priest, will be buried in two days."

"In the storm?"

"Yes."

"Because the stars say the time is right?"

I nodded.

"Heathenish!" the bishop said.

"You are invited."

Pedroza was silent.

"A number of slaves will be sacrificed," I said, feeling a

strong impulse to shock him out of his complacency. "Not so many as Chalco would desire were he alive, yet ample to see him and his small yellow dog safely across the river."

Pedroza reached for the doorknob, his beautiful ring flashing in the votive lights. I held him back with a hand on his arm. The cloth of his cassock was soft and of the finest weave.

"Since you are now in the land where men and women and children are sacrificed to the gods," I said, "you must come and be a witness so that you may go out in disgust and chastise the natives with long, fiery sermons."

"I don't have to be a witness in order to preach against this abomination."

"Bishop Pedroza," I said, "since you will not come to the burial by choice, I'll send guards to bring you. You will have a place in front of the godhouse, where you can watch everything that goes on — and much does. I will bring the Bible with me so it can be used."

I opened the door and stepped aside for the bishop to pass.

"What place," I said, "is more fitting to join the priesthood than the terrace of a Maya temple at sunset, before pagan thousands chanting the praises of Kukulcán, Feathered Serpent, Lord of the Evening Star! An irony seen but rarely, and then only in heaven, where God, I hope, looks kindly upon such things."

The bishop stepped past me. In the light of the votive lamps his face looked ghastly, yet he went down the corridor with swift strides, his heels clicking defiantly on the stones.

The storm lasted for two days. Then a hot land fog crept out of the jungle and covered the harbor and the city. Only the godhouse high on the Temple of Kukulcán rose above it, like an island in a sea. Word came that the Spanish fleet was anchored at a cove twenty leagues to the northwest and had lost one of its ships, apparently in the storm.

Pital, the new high priest, had charge of the burial rites. He was a softly spoken little man with a scraggly beard and a gentle gaze. I was surprised therefore to discover, when I reached the godhouse, that he was even more of a sun-worshipper than Chalco, the Aztéca. Instead of choosing a reasonable number to sacrifice, in addition to the seven slaves he had decided to sacrifice all of the Spaniards captured at Ixtlilzochitl. They now stood huddled together at the far end of the terrace.

Bishop Pedroza had refused to attend the burial and had barred his door against invaders. A messenger explained the situation to me as I watched the first of the burial rites, a solemn dusting of Chalco's remains with the plumes of a quetzal bird. I sent the messenger back with instructions to have the door removed and Pedroza borne to the godhouse by litter.

He appeared on the terrace, his hands bound, in the custody of two guards. I ordered him unbound.

His fine robe was ripped at the hem and his violet-colored vest awry. He didn't seem to be in a mood to listen to explanations, but I wanted him to know why he was here on the terrace of a Maya temple.

"Your Eminence," I said, "what you'll see now — the dusting of Chalco's remains with a quetzal plume you have missed, unfortunately, because it is a touching part of the burial rites — what you'll witness now may appear revolting."

Pedroza stood stiff-lipped and composed, his gaze averted from the scene around him — the godhouse decorated by gaping serpents and a hieroglyph of the sun, the terrace, its votive vases and the sacrificial stone, beyond the sea of fog that hid the crowd gathered below us in the square — to the fires of St. John the Baptist gleaming red on the far horizon.

"To the Maya," I said, "the sun is the source of all life. If it did not rise each day, they would live in a world of perpetual darkness lit only by the moon and the distant stars."

The bishop crossed himself. "God," he said, "is the source of all life. There is no other."

"The sun is God's creation," I said. "God, in one of His many forms, is the sun. The Maya deem it wise therefore to give the sun new strength after its long journey through the dark night and the gates of hell. Likewise, to give it new strength at sunset as it starts the long, perilous journey again."

"Barbarous," the bishop said, casting a glance toward the Spaniards standing miserably in the shadows of the godhouse. "Are these men to be victims of this abominable custom?"

"They are here to be sacrificed to the sun and the memory of Chalco, the Aztéca."

"You have the power to stop this sacrifice," Pedroza said.

"No, the power is in the hands of the thousands gathered in the square below us. Perhaps you could speak to them. You are familiar with the Maya language. You might persuade them."

Through the curtain of fog there rose a surging chant, now "Chalco," now "Kukulcán, Lord of the Evening Star."

"Speak," I said, "and tell the people that their rites are barbarous."

Pedroza looked about him helplessly, then raised his eyes to heaven.

"Yes, speak to God," I said. "Ask him to intercede for us. I have done so many times. Ask him! Since you are a bishop, since you are closer to Him than I am, certainly He will hear you."

"In His own good time God will attend to this outrage. But you, young man, have the power to stop it now. At this moment."

"And you," I said, coming to the subject that had not left my thoughts since I first had set eyes upon him, "have the power to make me a priest, an honor I desire with all my being. With a mere laying on of hands, you can do this."

"What there is to say, I've said," the bishop answered. "I will say no more except that in my eyes you are unfit for the office."

The fog was beginning to lift. There were brief glimpses of the crowd gathered at the base of the temple, who now as the godhouse came into their view increased their cries of "Chalco" and "Kukulcán."

The first of the Spaniards, a stout man with a grizzled beard, was placed on the sacrificial stone and held down. In an instant, not much after he had had time to cry out, his breast was slit open, his steaming heart was removed, held up to the crowd, then handed to a waiting priest who placed it reverently in a votive jar.

Pedroza had not uttered a sound. At the first sight of blood he had turned his back upon the scene. I repeated my humble request. He did not answer. He was staring at the heavens as if he expected a bolt of lightning to shatter the temple, stone from stone, to slay me where I stood.

Driven by a breeze from the sea, the fog was moving away. The upturned faces of the crowd were now visible. Pedroza strode to the edge of the terrace, to the balustrade of stone serpents, and flung out his hands. The crowd fell silent.

"Barbarians!" he shouted down to them, using his churchly Spanish. "Savages! Scum! Devil's scrapings from the gutters of hell! Enjoy yourselves while you have time. For God will not be mocked. Cortés, his faithful captain, will burn this temple to ashes. He will pursue you and ferret you out wherever you hide and burn you also."

The only part of the bishop's outcry that the crowd could have understood were the words "God" and "Hernán Cortés." But they heard his outraged voice and saw his violent gestures. An ominous silence settled upon them.

The priests in their dirty black gowns and long hair rank with spatterings understood no more than the crowd. But they too were silent. Pital, who stood a dozen paces away, clutching his obsidian knife, glanced at me. Finding nothing to stay his hand, he ordered the bishop seized and carried into the godhouse.

The Indians had begun to chant again, but now it was a wordless, threatening sound that came to my ears. The door of the godhouse opened and Bishop Pedroza was brought forth. They had taken away his cassock and violet-colored vest, even his fawnskin boots, and dressed him in a breech-clout with tassels.

Half-clothed, angular and thin, his high forehead whiter than ever, he still carried himself with dignity. He might have been fully dressed, a bishop waiting in the chancel to lead some holy procession. Pital reached out to take him by the arm, but, stared down by the bishop, he hesitated and turned to me.

Pedroza stood a dozen paces away. As I walked toward him, as our gazes met, I saw the same look I had seen before

— a steady, unblinking truculence that told me there was nothing more to say, no plea I could make that he had not heard already and rejected.

Deep in the temple the big drum sounded the hour of sunset. An afterglow, brighter than the blood that surrounded us, flooded the terrace. The cries from below had grown louder and more threatening. Pital was watching me, waiting for a signal, which, lifting my jaguar mask, I gave him.

Guards gathered the bishop in and placed him on the altar so that the stone bent his naked chest upward in a position that invited the knife. They held him there, two Indians at his feet and two at his head, courteously yet firmly, as if he were some winged serpent that might fly away at any moment.

I went to where he lay and looked down at him. He said nothing. Then he lifted a hand. For an instant I thought he intended to touch my brow. Instead, he touched his lips and then his breast, whispering to himself in Latin.

He calmly closed his eyes. He must have thought that all of this was an elaborate scheme to unnerve him, that I had brought him here to witness the savage rites, taken his cassock and vest away, had him dressed in an Indian breechclout, and placed him upon the sacrificial stone only to force him into granting my wish.

Pedroza opened his eyes and again our gazes met. I got down on my knees beside the stone in the blood of the Spaniard who had died to speed the sun on its journey through the perilous night and to ask the gods to befriend Chalco and his little yellow dog.

"You have heard my request many times," I said. "I ask it again."

"And it has been refused," Pedroza said calmly. "And I do so again."

There was no sign that he thought himself in danger. Impatiently he began to twist his amethyst ring, using his thumb to turn it round and round. I ordered the guard to release his hand.

"There is much work to do among these people," I said. "I can do it far better once I have received holy orders. I am handicapped now. The load is heavy. I strain under it."

No sound came from the bishop.

"Your Eminence, I beseech this favor!"

The bishop's eyes were closed. His lips were stiff and unmoving. He had sealed them. He had spoken the last word on the matter, confident that he was in the right. Confident, too, that I knew he was in the right.

Yet I was tempted to speak to him again. "You can hear the crowd clamoring for your life," I said. "You can see the high priest standing over you, anxious to use the sacrificial knife. This is not a play by Cervantes on a Seville stage nor a masquerade in the queen's garden. Once more I make the request."

There was no answer. He still twisted the beautiful ring round and round on his finger.

"Are you playing the role of a martyr?" I asked him. "Do you really seek martyrdom?"

Pedroza opened his eyes. He looked at me. It was only a glance, but in it, before he turned his gaze toward heaven, I read the answer to my question.

Pital, clutching the black obsidian knife in both his hands, peered down at me, waiting to use it. I put the jaguar mask on. I raised my fist and gave the signal.

That night, in the darkness, I went back to the godhouse and removed the amethyst ring.

Xico, the fastest and most trustworthy of my road weasels, arrived by sailing canoe shortly after dawn of the following day.

He brought word that two Spanish ships were anchored in a cove opposite the island, some nine leagues away. He had stumbled upon them by chance in the heavy fog that had settled on the coast during the night. Actually, he had sailed between the two caravels, close enough to hear the Spaniards shouting. When he did not answer them, they sent a round of shot through his sail.

Our enemies were unfamiliar with the coast. They had taken refuge from the fog and would not dare to leave until it lifted. When it did, probably within an hour or so, they would be able to sight the two landmarks they certainly had heard about and would be looking for — the Temple of Kukulcán and the fiery crest of St. John the Baptist. It was Xico's opinion that we could expect the Spaniards sometime before noonday.

With Flint Knife striding along behind me, I immediately set off to inspect our little army. In spite of the festivities, ending with Chalco's funeral, during which ample quantities of palm wine had been consumed, I found it in good shape. I alerted the captain of our fifty canoes, whose warriors were armed with spears, the guards at the main gate, and the cannoneers stationed on the walls to right and left, as well as the sailors aboard the *Delfín Azul.* The *Santa Margarita,* anchored far out at the entrance to the harbor, I could not reach because of the heavy fog.

The inspection took half the morning. As soon as it was over, I rode to the terrace, tethered the stallion, and took up a position on the roof of the godhouse, the highest point in the city, from which, once the fog had lifted, I would have a clear view of all the shorelines, the harbor, and the channel between the island and the coast.

To keep in contact with the *nacom,* I placed a squad of fleet-footed boys on the terrace, close at hand. When the fog began to lift I dispatched one of them with a message for the *Santa Margarita,* telling the dwarf that Cortés was on the coast, prepared to move against the island. Recalling how he had outwitted Emperor Moctezuma, I had already warned Cantú that he must not be allowed to enter the harbor under any pretext or excuse, and if necessary to block the entrance by sinking the *Santa Margarita.*

I waited impatiently for a clearer vision of the channel. Fog still hid the harbor, but beyond it there were now and then glimpses of open sea and the mainland coast. Nowhere did I catch sight of Spanish sails. It was possible that Cortés was not planning an attack upon the island. He had sent me no honeyed letters as he had to Moctezuma. No threats nor ultimatums. Perhaps because I myself would undertake such an attack were I in Cortés' shoes, I had concluded that it was something he would do.

The same misgivings that plagued me when I attacked Don Luis de Arroyo at Tikan plagued me now. The same rules of battle did not apply here — Caesar's dictum, *celeritas,* swiftness and surprise. At Tikan I had led an attack. Here I must repel one. Or did the rules apply equally to attack and defense?

In my mind, from the moment I discovered that Pedroza was a high-placed churchman and a friend of the Governor of Hispaniola, even to the last, when the two of us were enemies in a war of wills, I had harbored the thought of using him, should I ever encounter Hernán Cortés. But now Cortés was anchored across the strait only a few leagues away, and Pedroza lay dead.

I felt no remorse at Pedroza's death. He had hankered after it. He had courted it. He had willed it. In his cold eyes at the very last I had detected a glint of the ultimate vanity — a consuming desire for martyrdom. I had no doubt that he would achieve his desire. Someday his bones would be sorted out of the thousands stacked in the ossuary — not a difficult task, since they would be quite different from those of the Indians, especially the domelike skull — gathered up, and sent back to Spain, there to be decked out with flowers and worshipped by those who would never know that Pedroza was stubborn, truculent, and vain, a man so steeped in himself that he couldn't tell the love of ritual from love itself.

The temple drum sounded the midday hour. Though wisps of fog still drifted over the bay, I could make out the *Delfín Azul* tied at the wharf, her lombards and falconets trained westward, the flotilla of canoes between her and the harbor entrance. But the feathered poles that marked the entrance were barely visible. The *Santa Margarita* I could not find at all.

Sun shone in the channel and on the far blue line of the mainland coast. There was no sign of Spanish sails. Cortés might have passed us by and headed south for the shores of Guatemala and the river Polochic, where Moctezuma had told him in my hearing, not once but several times, that vast amounts of gold were to be found.

For most of a long hour, I stood on the roof of the god-house waiting for the harbor entrance to clear, to make certain that the *Santa Margarita* was in the right position if attacked. At last a messenger came clambering up the temple steps. He arrived on the terrace so out of breath that he could not speak, only raise his hand and point.

In the brief time I had watched him climb the stairs, the sun had burned away the last of the fog and the entrance stood clear. The *Santa Margarita* was not in sight. My first thought was that the dwarf had moved her to a different position. Possibly she had slipped her moorings and drifted away in the night or during the morning fog. I searched the harbor in vain.

"Where is the ship?" I shouted to the messenger. "The *Santa Margarita?*"

"Gone," the messenger shouted back, waving his arms to imitate a bird in flight. "Gone."

"Cantú, the dwarf?"

"Gone!" the messenger said.

The stallion was tethered at the far end of the terrace. Leaping to his back, I took the shortest of the three trails that led out of the temple, spurred him into a gallop when I reached the square, and rode pell mell for the harbor. Flint Knife was waiting for me on the deck of the *Delfín Azul.*

"I sent the message," he called down. "It is true. The dwarf has left. Two of our traders came from the north part of the island and said this. They were paddling along this morning. They were taking their time in the fog. A great white cloud rushed past them. It was whiter than the fog and had sails. It had a name, but it was not Maya and they could not read it."

The traders, who stood beside him, shook their heads.

"The *Santa Margarita* is gone," Flint Knife said. "It must have left around midnight. These traders were coming here. The ship was going the other way. It must be going to Hispaniola."

Flint Knife related all this in a toneless voice, stone-faced, calm, as though in the space of one night we had not been dealt a cruel and staggering blow. Half of our cannon were gone. Half of our muskets and gunpowder. Our best sailors were gone and our most experienced fighting men.

"I never liked the dwarf," Flint Knife said. "His eyes were too big. Like a woman's. And he made those sounds — he, he, he — like a monkey sitting up in the tree with more bananas hanging around than he can eat. This one did not cause me any surprise."

Nor was I surprised by what the dwarf had done, not really surprised. I was more surprised at myself for trusting him with a shipload of treasure worth millions and millions of *pesos de oro*. It was my fault to have put this great temptation in his way. If only he had chosen a better time to desert us!

The day steamed. Sweat ran down me in hot rivulets. "Move the *Delfín Azul* to the entrance," I said, more to show that I had not been rendered helpless by the bad news than by any faith in the procedure. "She is not so sturdy as the *Santa Margarita* and mounts lighter cannon. But we have no choice."

"What if we took up the marking poles from the channel?" Flint Knife said. "This Cortés does not know that we have a channel and that if you do not keep in the channel, then, bang, you go sailing onto the rocks."

"Good," I said. "And you take charge of the *Delfín Azul*. I'll go to the gate and back you up. We'll let Cortés find the channel for himself. If we're lucky he'll not find it and go aground."

"A *citam*. A pig."

"Yes, a wild pig who will try to root us out of our home."

"And eat us alive?"

"Yes, alive."

Hernán Cortés, in command of a ship under the banner of King Carlos the Fifth, in the name of the Holy Virgin, whose blessing he invoked before such encounters, came into sight in the early afternoon.

Watchmen on the godhouse roof announced his presence by three long blasts from their conch-shell trumpets. The winds were light, and more than an hour went by before the ship was visible from the deck of the *Delfín*. A second hour passed before the *Holy Virgin* appeared at the harbor entrance.

Cortés did not attempt the narrow passage. Instead, with a great clamor of voices and clanking of chains, the ship anchored squarely at the mouth of the channel. She was within a few short *varas* of where the line of markers began, the first of those we had removed in the hope of grounding all ships that tried to run the passage.

Flint Knife grunted. "How do these fellows know where to stop? The water is not clear. They cannot see to the bottom. They must have a soothsayer. What do you think, Lord of the Winds? You do not think? Well, I think so. Likewise, that we should give them some shots before long."

"Their guns are trained on the city," I said. "First, send messengers and order everyone indoors, especially the women. No one is to stay on the streets."

Messengers went out posthaste. A short time later Cortés

came ashore in a longboat, flanked by a guard of musketeers. He landed near the stern of the *Delfín* and came on foot to our gangway, the guard following in his wake. A standard-bearer preceded him, holding aloft a banner emblazoned with a gaudy crest.

Cortés looked much older than I remembered him, and more of a dandy in his red doublet with large white ruffs at neck and wrists. He recognized me at once, though I was wearing my jaguar mask and stood above him on the deck. He smiled, his lips curled nearly shut.

"We meet again," he said, "under far happier circumstances. Had I known when we met in Tenochtitlán that you were the king of La Ciudad de las Serpientes, I would have supplied you with a bodyguard and a more commodious dwelling." He bowed with a stiff, curt movement of his head. "I ask your forgiveness."

I ignored the apology. "You have come here for provisions?" I said. "You're in need of water and food? We have both."

"We are in need of both," Cortés said, "but before food and water, be it known to you that I have come from distant lands at the bidding of my emperor, Carlos the Fifth, and of his Lord and Protector, Jesus Christ."

I had heard these words before. He used them whenever he marched into an Indian village, speaking them by rote, from a long memory. Saying them now, he glanced from bow to stern with a practiced eye, counting the cannon, appraising the crew that served them, the numbers of men with muskets, slingstones, and javelins.

He straightened his white ruff and glanced up at me. "Be advised," he said, "that from this moment, henceforth and forever, La Ciudad de las Serpientes is a possession of the emperor, Carlos of Spain."

He paused, as I had often seen him do, to allow a guard

to sound a flourish on a small silver trumpet. Whereupon a volley of musket shots answered from the deck of his ship. Clouds of smoke rose up and drifted toward us.

I removed my mask. I waited until I caught his gaze, which had been shifting back and forth between the caravel and the warriors in plain view at the gate.

"Señor," I said, "this city and island and the seas that surround them are already in the possession of King Carlos. His Majesty took possession of them years ago. The day that I set foot upon these shores."

A flush appeared on the captain's pale cheeks. He spat on the stones and wiped his mouth on a handkerchief he took from his sleeve.

"You had no patent," he said, raising his voice from the monotone he had been using. "You had no license to claim *anything* in the name of the king. Not so much as a grain of sand on the beach."

He looked away, running his eyes over the *Delfín,* her masts and bulwarks, her name freshly painted on the stern.

"This is the caravel," he announced, turning to an officer behind him, whom I had not noticed before but now recognized as Pedro de Alvarado, the cruelest of his captains. "It fits the description I received from Governor Velásquez. It's the same ship that disappeared mysteriously a few days after reaching Yucatán."

Cortés turned away from Alvarado and looked at me. "This ship was stolen," he said. "Are you the thief?"

Flint Knife had understood none of the conversation, but when I was accused of thievery, as Cortés raised his jeweled hand and pointed at me, he whispered a quick warning.

"The *citam* gets ready to seize you. I can kill the pig before he takes one more breath."

Flint Knife had never seen the skills of these fierce swordsmen, who wore Damascus steel under their fine velvet doublets, who were unacquainted with fear.

"Hold off," I said. "These are not children who face us."

Cortés apparently knew nothing of the Maya language, for his expression did not change.

"On the ship that you stole," he said, "on whose deck you now stand, there was a distinguished passenger — Rodrigo Pedroza, Bishop of Alicantara, a dear friend of mine. I have recently learned from Governor Velásquez that he carried a message for me from King Carlos, whose purport I also learned. Having seized his ship, you must know what became of him."

Cortés had lowered his voice and was speaking now in the kindly tone I had heard him use with Moctezuma, with the Cholólans before he slew them and their blood sloshed in the gutters.

I didn't hesitate to answer. "Pedroza was here on the island for weeks. I saw little of him. He was a man who wanted to be by himself."

"Where is he?" Cortés said.

"He disappeared," I said. "He could be with the saints. He was a saintly man."

Cortés did not care for this remark. His bony cheeks took on a deeper hue — I marveled that the ruthless captain had not lost his ability to blush. His light-colored eyes searched me over, strayed off, and came back to focus on my hand.

"I observe that you are wearing a bishop's ring," he said. "I have been watching you as you twisted it on your finger. May I inform you that this holy ornament is not worn on the left hand and not on the third finger, but on the right hand and the fourth finger."

A chill ran through me. I had forgotten the amethyst.

"It reminds me of a ring Bishop Pedroza wore," Cortés went on. "It was unique. Unusual in shape. Cut squarely. I admired it when the bishop gave me his blessing on the day I set off on my voyage to Yucatán."

Cortés had described exactly the ring I was wearing.

"Pedroza owned many rings," I said. "He was vain about rings, also about clothes. He had clothes for every day. A chest full of clothes — surplices and cassocks and vests. And a little leather bag filled with rings."

"I've never heard this about him," Cortés said. "But you are right about his soul. It would be with the saints if he were dead. But he is not dead, and Governor Velásquez has charged me to find him."

"I'll be pleased to help you in your worthy search," I said.

"Pedroza, was he there when the ship was captured?"

"Yes."

"He was here on the island and then disappeared?"

"Yes."

Cortés mumbled something to Pedro de Alvarado, then started to say something to me, then thought better of it. After a moment he turned his back and strode away, followed by his captains and men, and climbed into the longboat, which sped off up the channel. A short while later the caravel raised anchor and sailed toward the south on a brisk wind.

"There are things I do not understand," the *nacom* said, disappointed that Cortés had run away without a fight, with not so much as a skirmish. "This man comes and talks and does nothing. His people carry weapons they do not use. The ships carry big thundersticks they point at us and do not fire. Then they flee like scared rabbits."

"Cortés has experienced much," I said. "He is a warrior. While he talked, he was busy counting our cannon, our spearmen waiting in the canoes. He studied the walls around the harbor, guessed at their height, counted their defenders, the ones he could see, knowing there would be double that number he could not see. He missed nothing. He decided we were ready for battle and that his chances of capturing the city were not good."

"He can change his mind," Flint Knife said, "and return."

That Cortés would return was certain. His hunger for gold had not been satisfied by the treasures of Tenochtitlán. The hunger of his men, upon whom victory depended, was insatiable. We mined no gold, yet he knew that we had it stored away in secret chambers and buried in ruined temples. He would not rest until it was found.

But more important, he had been asked by Governor Velásquez to find Pedroza. And just as important, to find and arrest me for crimes against the king. The governor's requests were commands. He ruled New Spain. He was the voice of King Carlos. And Cortés was well aware of his power.

"You have seen this Cortés before?" Flint Knife said. "In Tenochtitlán?"

"There and other places."

"I don't think you like him."

"No."

"And he doesn't like you."

I twisted the amethyst and said nothing. The ring felt like a burning coal.

Cortés was no sooner behind the headland than a blast of trumpets and a roll of drums announced that the funeral rites had begun once more. I put half the canoemen on guard and half the warriors at the gate and the wall embrasures. I left Flint Knife in command of the ship, rode back to the temple, and took my place among the priests.

Five Spaniards were yet to be sacrificed, Pital informed me.

"I am sorry," he said in his reedy voice, "that you could not collect a few more of these Spaniards. They have such beautiful white skins. Such fine big hearts, bigger than my fists. Our beloved friend and his yellow dog will have all the strength they need for the long journey."

Chalco, whom I had argued and fought with, lay dead under a blanket of green boughs. Before me, however, knife in hand, stood another high priest even more bloodthirsty. But it was not in my mind to argue with him over the five Spaniards. As minions of a ruthless king and a cruel master, they had killed thousands of innocent people. They had brought death. They had celebrated it in the name of Jesus Christ. They deserved to die. Then let them die! Let the squinting little priest wield his obsidian knife!

At sunset, after the rites were over, I rode back to the harbor, where Flint Knife gave me the startling news that Cortés was anchored in a cove some three leagues away, the same cove I had camped in for months after the shipwreck.

"It is reported," he said, "that they have fires on the beach. They are cooking supper and some of them are bathing in the lagoon."

"While they are having such a good time," I said, "we should fall upon them from the land and sea both. From the jungle and from the beach."

"The trail is dangerous at night," Flint Knife said. "We have brave warriors, but they do not care for this trail in the darkness. Spirits fly there. Many have been injured on this trail at night. Not killed, but have had their ears bitten off. I have seen these spirits. They are blind and have wings. Our warriors do not like to go on that trail when the sun leaves. If we make them, they will get frightened before they reach the cove, which is a bad way to start a battle."

"*Celeritas,*" Caesar had said. "Surprise and speed." And he had fought his victorious campaigns upon these simple ideas.

An excellent chance to capture Cortés lay before me. To descend upon him suddenly from front and rear — by canoe and by the jungle trail in the darkness lit by his own campfires — was an alluring prospect. But Flint Knife was a Maya and knew the Maya warriors. My experience with them was limited. At Tikan the battle had been won because the enemy ceased to fight when they learned that they were facing the god Kukulcán. The skirmishes at Uxmat and Zaya had been the same. I, therefore, followed his advice. And lest we ourselves be surprised, I posted extra watchmen on the trail and on the headlands.

Late in the afternoon three days later, sails appeared on the horizon. Farmers were still burning brush on the *milpas* and the smoke made it difficult to see. An hour or more must have passed before we made out that the sails belonged to a flotilla of six ships.

Shortly thereafter, to our consternation, Cortés' ship rounded the headland and joined them, and the seven formed a line that came toward us, swallow-tailed pennons flying, under sails marked by Spanish crosses.

"Seven!" Flint Knife said under his breath.

"But they can't find the channel," I said.

We were standing on the afterdeck of the *Delfín*. In silence we watched the Spanish flotilla come to anchor at some distance from the harbor entrance, out of range of our lombards.

One of their ships, led by an armed longboat, entered the channel, closely followed by a caravel flying Cortés' flag. Guided by the longboat, they threaded their way down the winding passage, then anchored in position squarely across it, thus blocking the *Delfín* from reaching the sea, should the need arise.

I heard no voices, no commands. The whole operation was done quickly and without a hitch, as if it had been done before. I was dismayed by its suddenness. We had lost our best weapon. We had removed all the channel markers, but to no avail. I was too shocked to give an order, or even to decide what order to give.

"Cortés must have someone in the longboat who knows the passage," I said.

"He captured someone," Flint Knife said. "A pearler or a fisherman. There are many who come and go."

The *Delfín* was a match for the two caravels, backed up as we were by a fleet of canoes manned by warriors armed with spears and slingstones. But the five sitting outside the entrance, ready to unloose a hundred heavy lombards, could overpower us with one brief salvo.

"Our warriors at the gate," I said to Flint Knife. "What can we expect from them? Will they stand against all these cannon and muskets?"

"Against Maya weapons, they will stand," Flint Knife said. "Only a few, those who fought at Tikan, have faced the sticks that thunder and those that belch fire."

"How many warriors will stand?"

"Two hundred."

"Who will run?"

"Hundreds. More, perhaps. Less, perhaps."

"Most of the army runs away? I counted on better."

"There are things you must think about, Lord of the Evening Star. One thing, the Maya are not the Aztéca. They are not warrior people. Once, many *katuns* ago, they fought everyone, also among themselves. Then Kukulcán came and taught them not to fight anyone or each other. When he left they remembered Kukulcán. Now you are back. They remember what you said once. Then you told them to be brothers to everyone. Now you tell them not to be brothers to everyone, chiefly to this Cortés and his white men. Now many of them wonder what to do."

"Now is not the time for wonder," I said.

There was no movement on the deck of either of the caravels, but on both ships the cannon were run out and ready. Cortés was studying us through a spyglass. Smoke from the burning fields veiled the sky, yet the sun was fiercely hot, and to shield himself he stood beneath an awning erected on the afterdeck, his odd-shaped cap on the back of his head.

I could read his mind. He could sink the *Delfín* with one blast of his cannon. This he did not wish to do. Not because the ship was valuable and belonged to Governor Velásquez, but because I was the quarry, the reason he was here in the harbor, sweltering under the fierce sun.

"My gunners are waiting," Flint Knife said. "And the canoes are waiting also."

"Let them wait," I said. "Let us all wait. I don't like the looks of the five caravels out there at the entrance. You'll notice that they have moved up while we've been talking and now we're within range of their lombards. Nor the two sitting over there gaping down our throats. How does all this strike you, *nacom?*"

The *nacom* fell into deep thought. His body, painted black and striped with white, glistened in the hot sun. He turned his back on the enemy ships and looked up at the soaring Temple of Kukulcán.

The longboat that had guided the Spaniards down the channel now came into view. In the bow stood Captain Alvarado in full armor, a bright plume in his helmet and a sword in his hand, which he was pointing toward the city. He was talking to someone, probably Cortés.

The longboat drew close, disappeared under our bow, and reappeared at our stern. Looking down from the ship's rail, I met the hard, black stare of Pedro de Alvarado. Partly hidden by his bulky frame was a figure wearing quilted armor and a cap with a feather, whom I took to be Hernán Cortés. Then the boat shifted with the tide, and I saw to my dismay that under the feathered cap was the upturned face of Doña Marina. Out of pride and emotion, thinking that I might be duped into surrendering, Cortés had sent her to present his demands.

She came up the gangway, followed by Alvarado and three soldiers carrying muskets. She had changed. There was no sign of the barefooted girl who had brought me food during those first wild days after the shipwreck. She was not the girl who had groveled at my feet in the garden of Moctezuma less than a year ago, unable to utter a word, so overpowering was my godly presence.

Not daring to look at me, Doña Marina met my gaze with a cold, sidelong glance. She meant to let me know that she no longer thought that I was the god Kukulcán. I swallowed my anger.

"Señor," she said, to make certain how she felt, "I bring a message from Hernán Cortés, Captain-General of His Majesty King Carlos, mighty sovereign of many lands and of New Spain and all its possessions."

"Cortés," I said, "was here two days ago with a message. I did not listen to it then. Nor do I listen to it now."

She ignored me and went on. "You are hereby informed that this island is a possession of King Carlos and that you are to give it over forthwith to Captain Alvarado, who has been sent here by Captain-General Cortés."

She spoke in rapid Spanish, running the words together — King Carlos was one word, *kinkarlos* — as if she had learned them by rote and didn't quite know what they meant.

"Would it not be better," I said, making an effort to hide my anger, "since you are a Maya, if you spoke in the Maya language?"

Color showed in her cheeks. She glanced at Alvarado, who stood stiffly beside her, a protector with a quick sword and, as I had learned in Tenochtitlán, a quick temper. She waited until he nodded approval.

"It was you," I said to her in Maya, "who guided the enemy ships safely through the channel. You have turned against your people. You have betrayed the city. For what reason?"

She took her time, thinking of an answer. She took off her pretty cap and brushed the feather and put it back on, all this deliberately, with the airs of a Spanish lady.

"Ceela Yaxche," I said, using her Maya name to remind her that for all her airs she was a Maya and not a Spaniard, "do you wish to let these murderers loose in our city? You saw what they did in Cholólan when they smeared the streets with blood. You were there at Texcála, I saw you, when Cortés cut off the hands of the old men. You were in Tenochtitlán and saw the temples burn and the man who stands beside you slay a hundred Aztéca nobles while they were happily dancing."

The faintest shadow crossed her face. "These were things that had to be done," she said. "Things, señor, that you have not done. The captain-general says that when he came and anchored in the bay he could see people being sacrificed at the temple. He could hear their cries and smell the blood. It was stronger than the smell of the sea, the blood was."

Again she glanced at Alvarado, who looked uncomfortable in the violent heat. He had not come to parley, but to state a simple demand.

"You stood on the terrace," she said, "and in the square and told people that it was wrong for them to offer hearts to the sun. They did not heed your words at all. They still do this and will never stop doing it until they are made to. It is Captain-General Cortés who will make them stop. He did with the Aztéca in Tenochtitlán and he will do it here."

"By killing people, killing them just to save their souls."

She crossed herself. "The soul is immortal," she announced.

"I see that you no longer worship Ix Chel, the moon goddess. You have become a Christian. Yes? Well, I am pleased. I didn't have much success with you, as I remember."

"You thought about your own soul too much," she said. "Then you thought about the city too much. You thought a lot, señor." She tossed her long black hair. "I like Tenochtitlán better than here. Here everyone goes around in poor clothes."

Alvarado had grown restless. He sauntered to the rail and looked down at the crowded longboat, then at the tower on the mainmast, where we had a lookout with a spyglass, at Cortés' caravel, anchored in the channel, then at the canoes filled with Maya warriors.

"Bastante," he shouted to Doña Marina. "Enough of this Indian talk. What does he say? Shall we begin to blow down the walls or shall we not?"

I had forgotten that I was faced with disaster. Alvarado's shout brought me to my senses. I drew Flint Knife aside.

"What do you think?" I asked him.

"I think we should kill this man," he said, "and those in the boat. We do not have forever. We should do it now. Later sometime we can think about Cortés."

Alvarado strode back and forth. He lifted his hot steel helmet and wiped the sweat from his brow. He was watching us.

Doña Marina said, "There are more ships coming. Three more with many soldiers. Let me take a good answer to Cortés. Otherwise he will blow up this ship and knock down the city stone after stone. Many people will die because you are proud and selfish. And God has forsaken you."

A Christian lecture! From an Indian neophyte! My blood boiled. I turned to Flint Knife with an order on my lips when Alvarado suddenly came between us. I thought for a moment that he was about to put a hand on my shoulder and reason with me, for he knew that the city was not helpless. He could see the fleet of canoes close at hand. There were men standing on the walls and hundreds, possibly a thousand, ready beyond the walls.

Instead of the friendly gesture I expected, in one deft movement Alvarado drew his sword from its sheath and thrust it deep into Flint Knife's chest.

An anguished, drawn-out cry came from the watchman high on the mainmast. Flint Knife staggered to the rail and raised his hands in a signal to the warriors waiting in the canoes. As I grappled with Alvarado, parrying a thrust of his sword, I was struck from behind, a crashing blow that sent me reeling.

Night had fallen. Through the port above my head I saw a misshapen moon in a black sky. Sails were flapping and I heard the creak of timber.

At first I thought that the ship was moving on a calm sea, but after a time, hearing the distant boom of the temple drum, I realized that it was still at anchor and the sounds I heard came from the running tide.

I must have slept, for through the port I now saw tumbling clouds and caught brief glimpses of the sun. Someone was at the door. I closed my eyes, feigning sleep, thinking that whoever it was would leave. When I looked up again, the door was open and Cortés stood at the foot of my bunk.

"The city is quiet," he said. "I sent Doña Marina ashore at dawn. She returned with an interesting story."

My head was bursting. I could not focus my eyes on anything in the cabin.

"What I am about to relate," Cortés said, "is important. You miss it at your peril. Are you listening?"

"I listen as well as my head permits."

"You are fortunate to have a head. Alvarado was instructed to bring you here alive, but one of his aides lost his wits and almost, nearly . . ."

Cortés had not come alone. I made out the figures of two men, one of them carrying a lantern, the other, a chain slung over his shoulder. The lantern light hurt my eyes.

"Again I remind you to listen," Cortés said. "Doña Marina went to the temple at dawn. She was very helpful. She talked to the elders. She told them that you, the god Kukulcán, had left the island as you had left it once before, long ago. And that you would return, not in your present guise of a tall, blond youth, but as an elder, wise with the experience of age."

The man dumped the chain he was carrying. It was heavy and made a clatter. His companion turned up the lantern, put it on the floor, and stepped away to avoid the heat.

Cortés said, "So you need not worry about the welfare of the Indians. They are in my care and will be treated kindly, as I treated the Indians of Tenochtitlán." He spoke with feeling, as if he really believed every word. "Except for those that deserved punishment."

He waved a lacy handkerchief, heavy with scent, under his nose, then called to the guard, who came forward with his lantern and held it at arm's length, close to my face.

"Before when we talked," Cortés said, "I asked about Bishop Pedroza. You replied that he had been here on the island but had disappeared. You said that if he were dead he would be with the saints. An evasive answer. You also said that you would be pleased to help me find him. Where, señor, shall we look? Where shall the search begin? Here? Now?"

I winced and turned away from the searing heat. "Ask the high priest. Ask Pital," I said. "He will know."

The man at the door picked up his chain, sauntered across the cabin, and stood behind Cortés.

"This high priest," Cortés said. "Where is he?"

"In the temple. He is always there. He lives there," I said.

"Hold the lantern closer." Cortés bent down to examine my hand. "I observe," he said, "that you still wear the amethyst ring."

The lantern came closer. Big and made of iron, it burned my flesh.

"Pedroza's ring!" Cortés said. "I see the stone is beveled where it meets the band. And etched with a cross."

His voice sounded from far off, from outside the cabin. I tried to answer, but choked on the words.

"The iron fist," Cortés said. "Bring it. We'll get an answer."

I remember that the guard dropped the chains, that he felt around in his tunic, then passed something to Cortés. I remember that I tried to make an unyielding fist but failed. The iron hand clamped shut on me.

I remember nothing else until later when it was night again. I wasn't sure whether it was the night of the second day or the third.

It must have been the pain that brought me awake. My arm throbbed with pain, my whole body throbbed, but my hand was on fire. Then vaguely I began to wonder if I still had a hand. People who had lost some part of their body — an arm or a leg or a hand — felt at first and even later that it had not been lost, that it was there yet, waiting to be used.

I reached down and felt around. It was there, twice the size of my other hand, still doubled up into a hard, unyielding fist. On my finger was the amethyst ring.

Through the deadlight I could see a storming sky. Rain beat on the cabin roof and ran in the scuppers. Drops of water were falling on my bunk, one slow drop at a time, from a seam overhead.

I struggled up from the bunk and, finding that I could walk, went to the door and put my ear against it. I heard nothing except the running water and a stiff wind in the rigging. Then I opened the door a crack.

The catwalk leading into the cabin was deserted, as was the deck below. But after a moment I heard voices. I shut the door and went back to my bunk. By the feeble light of a lamp swinging in the gimbals, I noticed a tray of food that someone had set on the floor while I was asleep. It looked gray and old and turned my stomach.

While I was sitting there, perhaps an hour later, in pain and fear, knowing that Cortés and his bullies would return at any time that suited them, with a rush of wind the door suddenly opened, then quickly closed. Doña Marina stood there, her long hair wet and windswept. She held her fingers to her lips in silent warning.

She said, "Do as you are told, señor. Guards are on the deck. They are everywhere except by the stern. Ayo is by the stern with a canoe. Ayo is the one who took Don Luis and me across to the mainland. That was the night we fled. In the corner behind you is a crawl-through. It leads to the rudder."

I started to speak. I wanted to ask a hundred questions.

"Go," she said. "They are coming back for you. They will be here before the night is over. They have a place for you where they can hang you upside down by your feet. Cortés has found the bishop's body and he is very angry. He is angrier than I have ever seen him."

Again I started to speak. She had gone. I watched her run along the catwalk, climb down the ladder, and disappear in the rain, her long black hair streaming.

I closed the door. I stood there, unable to move. Moments passed. I roused myself, fearing that by now the Indian and his canoe would be gone, and found the crawlway — I knew where it was because Cortés' ship and the *Santa Margarita* were built alike. It led to a cramped space, mostly taken up by the arm that worked the rudder. Where it was attached to the rudder, below the gudgeon that it turned upon, was a space large enough to squirm through. The broad face of the rudder was strapped with iron bands. On these slim projections I must lower myself.

The rain had lessened but the wind blew strong. Grasping the rudder's edge, I climbed out on the first of the straps. I saw nothing below except black water. The canoe could be hidden under the ship's counter. It might have gone.

Lowering myself one strap at a time, I had gone only half

the distance when a gust of wind swept me into the sea. I went under and after an endless time came up. A hand reached out of the darkness and clutched my hair.

A frightened voice, which I recognized as the voice of the young priest Ayo, humbly said, "I beg your forgiveness, Lord of the Wind of Knives, for grasping you in this unseemly way. But I fear that you will drown unless I do so."

"Hold on!" I shouted.

Inching along on his knees, a helper appeared out of the gloom, and among the three of us I managed to scramble over the side.

Ayo took up his paddle. "We cannot stay here," he said. "Where, Lord of the Evening Star, do you wish to go? In which of the Four Directions?"

I sat silently in the bottom of the canoe, bilge water sloshing over my legs, aware that any moment we might be discovered, yet powerless to decide what I should do. There was a chance I could rally the warriors and drive Cortés from the city. Perhaps I had more than a chance.

"What has become of my warriors?" I said.

"They are scattered," the young priest said. "When the *nacom*'s body toppled into the sea they lost spirit. When you fell on the deck and lay quiet, as though you were dead, they laid down their weapons."

"I will ask them to take up their weapons again."

"The white soldiers roam the city. They ride around on big deer, carrying thundersticks, with big dogs running along beside them."

"I can gather warriors. They outnumber the white soldiers. They will answer if I call them. We will gather in the jungle secretly."

"It is too late for gatherings."

"Why?" I said angrily. "Are you carrying on my feud with Chalco? Are you my enemy?"

"I have always been your friend," Ayo said, hurt by my

words. “Otherwise, King of the Wind of Knives, I would not be here in the storm, in danger of my life.”

Rain was falling again. The city was a vast black shadow. A single fire showed on the godhouse roof.

“As a friend,” I said, “you doubt that the warriors will answer me?”

“You can see that the streets are deserted,” Ayo said. “The citizens are hiding. Farmers have gone back to their farms. The temple fires are out, all save one. The people mourn.”

“They have much to mourn. Flint Knife’s death. My wounding. The temporary loss of the city. This and more.”

“Yes, much, but it is your leaving that truly grieves them.”

“I haven’t left. I am here, waiting.”

“We are all waiting,” Ayo said, “and it is a bad thing. Let us go away from the ship and take our chances elsewhere.”

We moved out into the channel against the tide, slowly because the canoe was heavy — fashioned as it was from a hollowed log — and half full of water. I began to bail, using my good hand.

“The people grieve because they think you have left the island,” Ayo said. “They thought you were dead when they saw you lying on the deck and you did not move and were carried away. They thought that the white men had hidden your body. Then Ceela Yaxche went to see the three elders and high priest Pital. She is called Doña Marina now. And she has changed. She is no longer a Maya. Now she calls herself a Christian woman and has a string of beads with a cross around her neck. She is different now, very important, but she is still a Yaxche and my cousin. She said to them that you had not been killed. You were alive. Then after three days . . .”

“I was on the ship three days?”

“For three days and three nights,” Ayo said. “Then Ceela told them that you had disappeared. In the middle of the night you had sailed away on a snakeskin raft, like the raft you had when you left before. Only this time you said that when you came back you would be in a different form. Not young as now. You would be an old man with much experience who would bring them many beautiful gifts."

We moved up the winding channel to the entrance, past the first of the anchored ships. We were close enough to be hailed. We didn't answer. A musket shot struck the water behind us, but we did not stop. By the light from their stern lantern, I caught a glimpse of the young priest. His looped earrings glittered. His face was serious, and when I looked at him he averted his eyes.

"Where is the snakeskin raft?" he said. "In the cove by the volcano?"

"You think that it is time to go?" I said.

"Three days now," Ayo said. "The night they carried you away, there was a great fire in the volcano. Seven fiery flowers burst out of its mouth, one after another. They filled the sky. It was a sign to us all, given by you, Lord of the Winds."

I sat in a canoe within sight of the city, injured but alive, yet to the priests who read the signs of the fiery flowers and the people to whom they were reported I had sailed away as I had done before, long centuries in the past. Even to the young priest kneeling scarcely two arm's lengths from me, I was only a shadowy presence.

The fire on the godhouse roof was dying out. Gray shadows covered the white stones of the terrace. Only a short time ago — was it two years or three? — I had stood there with Cantú the dwarf, looked out upon the ruined city, and dreamed of gleaming temples, of a port that sheltered caravels from all the ocean seas, of high walls built to withstand every foe, of treasures wrested from the tyrants of a hundred towns.

We passed the last of the enemy ships. The fire on the godhouse roof had died out. The city was now dark. The only light came from far away, from the burning crest of St. John the Baptist, whose name I had used and whom, in pride and lust, I had failed.

We raised a sail when the enemy ship fell astern and reached the coast at dawn, after a stormy night. Having seen this part of the coast in the past, I chose a sheltered place to land, much like the cove where I had been tossed on the beach years ago in the wreck of the *Santa Margarita.*

"The snakeskin raft?" Ayo said as we parted company. "Do you wish me to wait until it comes?"

"It may be days," I said.

He took a handful of cacao beans from his gown. "You may need these on your journey," he said.

I was about to refuse them, then thought better of it. I was no longer a god. Wherever fate took me, I would need money.

"I always planned," I said, accepting the dark little nuts, "to make money out of gold, as they do in Spain. Coins they call them. *Ducados, pesos, castellanos.*"

"You can do this when you return someday," the priest said.

"There are many things to do if I return, but this will not be the first."

Ayo bowed, touching his forehead to the sand. He got into the canoe and put up the sail. Only then did he wave farewell. I watched him for a long time, until he disappeared in the sun.

I stood on the shore alone. The sky had cleared. Heat came out of the jungle in breathless waves, and already the sun shimmered like brass.

On the far horizon St. John the Baptist glowed red. As its fiery crest sent forth clouds of smoke that drifted down upon the city, I was assailed by a bitter thought: if only it would erupt and bury the island beneath a mountain of burning lava. Yes, all of the island — the jungle and the bay where the Spanish caravels were smugly anchored, triumphant Cortés and his captains. Yes, the whole ungrateful city itself — yes, and the thousands who had witnessed my humiliation. All buried deep beneath mountains of fire!

I stood for a time, gazing about at the unfamiliar beach and the jungle that came down to meet it. I was hungry — from what Ayo told me, I had not eaten for three days and nights. I saw nothing that was dry enough to use for a fire and nothing to cook if I had one.

A small, clear stream ran past me, much like the stream that ran in the island meadow where I was cast away. There would be fish, but I couldn't catch them. And fish in the sea. As before, I satisfied my hunger with wild fruit, which grew everywhere in profusion.

Having eaten, I fell asleep, awakened at sundown to eat, then slept through the night, ate again, and again went to sleep. I had been carrying a heavy stone on my back. It was gone. I prayed each morning, but half-heartedly and without redeeming thoughts or wishes.

I followed these habits for a week and more — it might have been longer, even three weeks or a month, since I had lost count of the days. I began to have scattered thoughts about my future.

I even thought of returning to the City of the Seven Serpents. By now Cortés would have rifled it of its gold — what little the dwarf had missed — and left a small garrison behind, which could easily be destroyed. In time, however, he would return to take revenge on the city as he had upon Tenochtitlán. He would burn the godhouse, take down the Temple of

Kukulcán stone by stone, and with the stones build a Christian church.

Should I have done so? I had a guilty feeling that I should have, beginning on my first day in the city. And that despite all his brutalities, Cortés was right in not trafficking with the devil and I was wrong. In my stubborn, prideful way, I had even sat down and dined with Satan.

The thought of returning was an aberration, born of wounded pride and stubbornness. Especially the latter. I had always been stubborn. I had drunk it in with my mother's milk. I recalled the time it had nearly cost me my life.

That was when we moved from Seville to the village of Anazo. I was eight years old. We had lived on the banks of the Guadalquivir, but the river ran deep there, so I was never allowed to swim. Upstream, however, at Arroyo, it wasn't deep, and boys went swimming there in the summer.

The first week I was in the place, some of my new friends came by and asked me to go swimming. Which I did — after my mother made me promise that I wouldn't go into water that was over my head.

Most of the river ran shallow, but there was one deep pool. Just before we started for home, all the boys jumped in. They went down one after the other into water that was over their heads. I saw them touch bottom. They came up, waded out, and waved for me to jump.

I hesitated. I had told them, when we first got to the river, that I could swim. I even bragged a little, saying that I had learned when I was only four years old.

There they were, six of them, shouting for me to jump. And here I was on the bank, stiff with fear, unable to swim so much as a foot. I stared down into the deeps, scared to death. But certain that I would rather drown than go back on what I had said, I jumped.

I don't remember how I escaped. I guess by instinct, as a

dog paddles. But I do remember that my friends fished me out and that I was full of water when they laid me on the bank. I also remember my mother hovering over me, clutching her black shawl, weeping in joy and fright.

"It's that stubborn streak," she said, when she was over her fright. "You would rather be stubborn as a pig and drown yourself . . ."

The scene faded. The aberration had been a brief one. What I had failed to do on the Island of the Seven Serpents in times of peace I had no chance of ever doing now. Certainly not now that I had incurred the wrath of Governor Velásquez. I had eluded Cortés, but the governor would send other men to track me down.

With its abundant fruit and stream of fresh water, the cove was not inhospitable. I had made a rough shelter among the trees, out of sight of the many passing canoes, yet for all my caution I might be discovered. The season of fruit would soon come to a close. I had no fire and no prospects of building any until the daily downpours ended with summer. A sensible course was to move south along the coast — the northern coast was already overrun by Spaniards — away from the Island of the Seven Serpents.

I remembered the village of Chichén-Palapa, and its cacique, Matlazingo, who liked Spaniards. But how was I to reach this friendly village?

It lay at a distance of more than sixty leagues — the *Santa Margarita* had taken two days to get there, not counting the storm. There were no trails, at least none that I knew of. And if there were, if I found one, it would be dangerous for a white man. I could only travel by sea. But I didn't own a canoe, not even a raft.

Enormous trees grew to the water's edge, but I lacked an ax to fell one and the fire to hollow it out. I considered a raft, the kind Kukulcán had made. The jungle teemed with snakes, large ones, some five or six strides in length. I could fashion a frame of thin withes and cover it with snakeskins.

I settled on a raft made from trees that grew along the edge of the jungle. The wood was exceedingly light, easy to cut and move about.

Using shells sharpened to a fine edge with sand, I cut four dozen logs of a good length, bound them together with wet reeds, laying down four rows, one on top of the other, in opposite directions. I wove a small sail of split reeds, as I had seen the weavers do in the city square, and made a rough sculling oar.

It took me the rest of the summer to finish the raft. I would have finished it much sooner had it not been for my crippled hand. Cortés' iron claw had squeezed it like a vice. The wounds had healed, but it was now somewhat misshapen, the amethyst ring embedded in my finger. I would have taken the ring off had I been able to, for it constantly reminded me, as I worked, of Bishop Pedroza, that vain pedagogue who longed for saintly glory, whose memory I tried to forget.

The summer storms had ended. Early on a bright morning I sculled out of the cove and with the wind astern set sail for Chichén-Palapa. I was glad to be leaving my jungle camp.

With me I took the results of many hours of thinking. As I hacked away at the logs to make my raft, while I lay in bed at night, I had come to two conclusions.

Cortés was right when he burned the heathen temples, gathered up the bare stones, and from them built Christian churches. There was no other way, it seemed, though years would pass and generations would live and die before the Maya and the Aztéca forgot their pagan gods.

Perhaps Cantú the dwarf was right, also. He had played a scurvy trick upon the Maya. He had deserted me at a time when I needed him the most. Yet he had been sorely tempted. Gold was power. He would return to Seville and purchase a fine estate and a dukedom. He would dine with nobles, converse with the leading artists, philosophers, and men of science. He would sit with princes of the church and receive their churchly blessings and benefits. Cantú would revel in all this splendor while I, cast away for the second time in my short life, penniless and rejected, deserted by God, faced an uncertain future.

Yet I could blame no one for my plight. Who, I asked myself, had called upon me to do Christ's work? What voice had spoken? Who had chosen Julián Escobar to journey into pagan lands to save heathen souls? To fail, to find himself far from home, a fugitive hunted by the king's men?

I never glanced back at my jungle camp as the raft left the shore, or at the city that lay somewhere to port, or at St. John the Baptist, which had not erupted and buried the island as once I had wished it to do. I looked straight before me and made a silent vow.

Never out of sight of land and only by day, I sailed for close to three weeks. I was passed by many canoes, hailed by some, but mostly ignored. On another bright morning I entered the estuary that led to the village of cacique Matlazingo.

The cacique was lounging on the beach, in much the same position as I had left him months before, chewing on coca leaves and spitting in the sand. He recognized me at once, though this time no cannon had announced my arrival. I was stepping ashore from a raft, instead of from a longboat rowed by dozens of painted warriors. The sun had bleached my hair white and given my skin a mahogany hue. The diet of fruit had reduced my frame to skin and bones. Yet he greeted me with a Spanish *embrazo* — he must have learned the embrace from Gerónimo de Aguilar — so moved by emotion that he could scarcely speak.

"What great misfortune has overtaken you?" he managed to ask.

"A wrecked ship," I said, which was a statement not far from the truth. "I am the only survivor of a wrecked ship."

"The big one? The one that carried thunder and lightning?"

"Another one. Bigger. Much bigger."

"Very sad," Matlazingo said, shaking his head and offering me a sheaf of coca leaves. "These will help you forget the sadness."

"Food will help me more," I said.

At a click of his tongue it came, platters of food — berries, fruit, more fruit, bowls of chili pepper and *frijoles,* raw fish, corncakes, tall stacks of corncakes. I ate in silence, but not much, since my stomach had shrunk during the long summer and the food did not taste as good as I had expected.

"You will remember," I said, "that when I came here before, months ago, I spoke about a Spaniard."

"Yes, his name was Cortés," the cacique said. "I remember him. Hernán Cortés."

"Has he been here?"

"No, I have not seen this great man."

"Have you heard anything about him?"

"Much," Matlazingo said. "A little. A big canoe came, not big like yours, but big. It was filled with Spaniards. They were looking for gold. I told them I had no gold. They were not happy about this. But I gave them a basket of pearls and they felt happier. I asked them about this one you told me about."

"Hernán Cortés."

"Yes. They said he was with the Aztéca in Tenochtitlán. That is a place high in the mountains."

"I know where it is."

"The men said that he had been in trouble with the king, but he was not in trouble anymore. Now he is the cacique of everything." Matlazingo spread his arms wide, seemingly to take in the world.

If Cortés had returned to Tenochtitlán, given up any plans

of moving down the coast — news that had the ring of truth — then I was in no immediate danger. I queried the cacique further, trying to make sure that he wasn't dreaming. As future events were to prove, he was not.

Cortés had indeed been forced to hurry back to the Aztéca capital. His numerous enemies, including the powerful Bishop of Burgos, who accused him of taking one fifth of the booty as a captain and another fifth as king, had asked Carlos the Fifth to call him back to Spain. Instead, the young monarch had made him the governor, captain-general, and chief justice of all the Indies. He was now in Tenochtitlán, there to consolidate his new power and to plan new campaigns.

"Too bad," Matlazingo said. "Now I will never see the great Spaniard, Hernán Cortés."

"He travels much, honorable cacique. You may see him yet," I said.

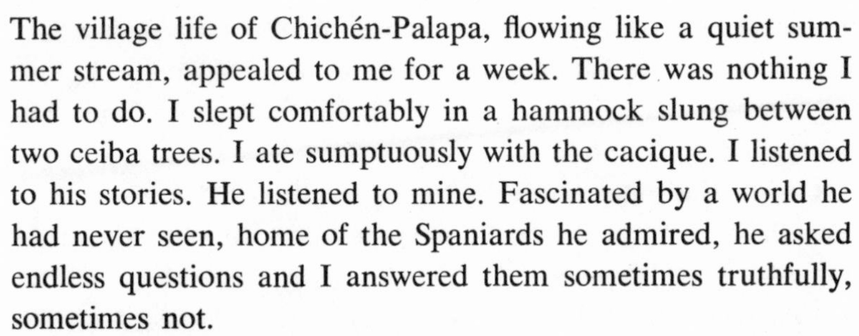

The village life of Chichén-Palapa, flowing like a quiet summer stream, appealed to me for a week. There was nothing I had to do. I slept comfortably in a hammock slung between two ceiba trees. I ate sumptuously with the cacique. I listened to his stories. He listened to mine. Fascinated by a world he had never seen, home of the Spaniards he admired, he asked endless questions and I answered them sometimes truthfully, sometimes not.

I had only two temptations during this time. While walking among the ruins of what was once a flourishing city, I was visited by the urge to restore its temples and public structures. The urge did not last. The Indians, like those I had lived among for years, seemed to lack any desire to bring back ancient glories. They were content to farm their few acres, fish in the sea, and worship their heathen idols.

The second temptation came one evening while I sat watching them emerge from their huts to wander around the village. I was tempted to sing the beautiful Salve Regina. The temptation lasted no longer than the first, as memories of my failures on the Island of the Seven Serpents flooded in upon me.

Before another week had passed, I grew restless. Taking note of my condition, the cacique suggested that I assume some of his duties as a medicine man and soothsayer. I was no longer white-skinned, but I was a blond Spaniard two *varas* tall.

"Everyone," the cacique said, "thinks that you were a speaker before somewhere. They want you to speak words to them."

"I've been a speaker," I said, "and did not like it."

"You may like it better in Chichén-Palapa."

"Less."

"You might go with the pearlers and dive for pearls. You are so tall you can stand on the bottom and need not dive."

The pearling season began with the end of the summer *chubascos* and lasted a month. Early on the last day of diving, as we were anchored at the mouth of the estuary, a ship flying a Spanish pennon sailed into our midst. Its captain appeared at the rail, stared down at us for a while, and then demanded gold.

One of the Indians offered him a handful of pearls.

"I have them," the captain shouted in clumsy Maya. "I come for gold."

"There is no gold," the Indian said, speaking the truth — during my weeks in the village I had seen none, in any shape. "No gold."

Smoke was rising at the far end of the estuary. The captain pointed.

"You have gold there?" he shouted.

The Indian shrugged, not understanding him. I understood but kept silent, and the ship sailed off toward the village. When we got back the captain was on the beach talking to Matlazingo, surrounded by a troop of his men. To frighten the Indians, he had brought three horses ashore and a pair of big staghounds.

I was close enough to hear most of the heated words, but out of sight. The captain, who was swarthy and stout, kept walking back and forth, facing the cacique, then turning his back upon him, talking all the while.

"I've been in this place long enough," the captain said. "I

ask you much. You answer nothing. The same always. You shake the head and say nothing. *Nada. Nada.*"

Matlazingo was bewildered. He quit chewing on his coca leaves and did not ask for more. He had met a Spaniard who wasn't like me or Gerónimo de Aguilar.

"My ears grow tired of hearing *nada, nada,*" the captain said. "Once more today I ask, where is the gold?"

Matlazingo glanced around in desperation. I believe he was looking for me, thinking that I could help him. But there was no way I could persuade the Spaniard that the cacique was telling the truth. And to walk out and face his inquisitor would put me in a dangerous situation. How could I tell if the captain wasn't one of Cortés' men, instructed, as he sailed down the coast searching for gold, to keep a weather eye out for me! I pressed back farther into the trees.

I heard nothing now of what was said between the two men, but I did see Matlazingo hold out a cluster of pearls, the Spaniard move his lips disdainfully, strike the cacique's outstretched hand, and scatter the pearls on the beach. He shouted at two of his men, who sprang forward and bound the cacique by his long hair to the tail of one of the horses. The horseman then spurred his mount into a gallop and dragged Matlazingo to the end of the street and back.

"Where do you hide the gold?" the captain asked.

Matlazingo lay on his side, covered with dust, still bound to the horse's tail. His bleeding lips formed a word, but he had difficulty saying it. The captain waited. He even stooped down to hear what the cacique had to say. What he heard displeased him, for at once he gave a sign. This time the horseman dragged Matlazingo toward the village square.

Meanwhile, the troops collected wood on the beach and built a fire. When the cacique was dragged back, they untied him from the horse's tail and tossed his limp body into the flames. The captain then glanced about for other Indians to torture, but everyone had fled. He called his troops together, roundly cursed the village, and went back to his ship.

That night, after the Spaniards had left, the Indians came back from hiding and we buried Matlazingo's ashes in one of the temples. The village mourned for a week and a day. At the end of that time I was asked to take the cacique's place as leader and medicine man, which, as courteously as I could, I declined to do.

Soon afterward one of our sailing canoes left Chichén-Palapa with a cargo of pearls to sell at a trading center three hundred leagues to the south. Though it caused the Indians much distress, I left with it, for I had lost my interest in the village since Matlazingo's death.

We arrived at Quintana after a week of good weather, in time for the opening days of the fair. The pearls, which were communal property, everyone owning a share in them, could have been sold out the day we arrived, but the Indians had come a long way and did not want to turn around and start back already. They wished to visit with old friends, take time with the bartering, and leave not a day before the last pearl had been sold. While this was going on, I decided I liked the town and the traders and travelers that came to it from everywhere in Maya country. I took my share of the profits, which were small, and stayed on when the canoe sailed home.

Quintana was located at the mouth of a tidal estuary, at the meeting of two large rivers. Its main street ran for half a league along a sandy strip between the rivers.

Some of it was taken up by guarded warehouses where the rich traders stored costly goods like ocelot skins and cloaks made of hummingbird feathers, but mostly it was filled with thatched arcades filled with stalls owned by the poor. The poorer yet spread blankets on the ground on both sides of the walkway that wound down the middle of the street.

RETA E. KING LIBRARY
CHADRON STATE COLLEGE
CHADRON, NE 69337

Beside this walkway in front of one of the warehouses, I spread my own blanket. Unsure of what I wished to sell, and what would sell, I bought a variety of things that I thought might appeal to children — like noisemakers, dolls, clay animals, toy spears, and slingshots. It was a small beginning.

On the first day, because my long legs, sun-bleached hair, and blue eyes attracted the children, I sold merchandise to the value of six cacao beans, half of it profit, valued in Spanish money, as close as I could figure, at some sixty *maravedís*. On the second day I did even better, and on the third day ran out of stock.

Whereupon the weathered old woman squatting on a blanket next to mine asked me to help her sell the straw hats she was weaving, which I did. Business was so brisk with the hats that she suggested we discard our blankets and open a stall with a roof.

"Then you can stand behind a counter like a true seller," she said, smiling a toothless yet engaging smile. "And then you will not have to sit on a blanket like an old woman."

"You only weave seven hats a day," I reminded her. "That's not enough hats to do business in a stall."

"I will find more weavers. Two more. Three. And I will make hats in all colors, like the rainbow. And not for women only, but for men and children, too. And you can stand up and sell them."

The prospect of standing on my feet appealed to me — after two days of squatting on a blanket, I could hardly walk — so we bought a stall in a good location and went looking for weavers. The old woman — her name was Zoque — took me up the street to the slave market.

"Two big canoes came with slaves," she said, "but now they are picked over. I want a young black one. You can teach them and they do not eat so much as the Indians eat."

There were ten slaves in the stockade, two of them black

women from Africa and the rest women from an island to the south.

Zoque chose one of the blacks, a handsome, muscular woman nearly as tall as I. I decided against her and tried to make a choice between a smiling, middle-aged woman of a happy disposition and a girl, scarcely a woman, although she held a child by the hand, so tightly that the child's fingers had turned white.

The mother's eyes were fixed upon some distant place, beyond the log platform she stood upon, the crowd that surrounded her, and the sharpened poles of the stockade. But the child gazed wonderingly at me, fascinated by what she saw.

The slave owner came to them last among those he was selling. "Sola Mulamé," he said, turning the woman around so she could be observed from all sides, "is twenty-five, a good worker, and docile by nature. Her daughter, Selka, is twelve years old, and very healthy."

Selka, on the contrary, was very sickly looking, with arms and legs like sticks, hip bones that pushed out against a cotton shift too small for her. The owner began to turn the child to show her off. She was gazing at me with black, unblinking eyes when he began and she was still gazing at me when she faced me again.

The old woman didn't care much for either of them. "The mother looks lazy," she said. "The girl will die before the year has gone."

A lordly Indian with a beautiful quetzal plume in his cap shoved forward and offered thirty cacao for the mother — for various reasons, he did not want the daughter. I paid the slave owner sixty cacao beans for both.

I had come to the mart out of curiosity, to humor the old woman — with no intention of buying slaves. Yet here I was the owner of two. Did I see something in the child's eyes? Did they mirror the depths of a Christian soul? Troubled, I took her and the mother away and left them with Zoque, who started that day to teach them the art of weaving.

They learned quickly, and within a month a steady stream of hats of all colors and sizes flowed onto our shelves. The trading center attracted crowds during fairs and fiestas, but there were always visitors on the street and, in a country of fierce sun and torrential rain, always a demand for hats.

During these first weeks Selka and her mother worked in the old woman's hut and I didn't see the child. I thought about her, however, wondering if it would be any use for me to instruct her in the Christian faith. Whenever the thought came to me, I remembered my failure with Ceela Yaxche — yes, with thousands of others — and promptly put it out of mind.

During one of the big fiesta weeks the old woman set the two weavers up in front to attract people who liked to watch other people work. The girl had changed. Her arms and legs were no longer sticks. Her hip bones didn't show anymore. The only thing that hadn't changed about her were her eyes. They still were black and unblinking. They sought me out — she had learned to weave without looking — whenever I was around. They followed me everywhere.

The day the fiesta was over and sales had slackened, I took her aside, tempted again, yes, again!

"Selka," I said, "you worship the sun god and Itzamná, the god of learning, and now that you are a weaver, Ix Chebel Yax, the goddess of weaving. But there is another god mightier than they. He towers over them as the ceiba tree towers above the saltbush."

"Where does this god live?" she asked, watching me warily.

"In the sky. In your heart."

She touched her breast. "Here?" she asked.

"There. In your heart and your mother's heart. And in mine. He lives everywhere."

"He is very busy," she said, "to be everywhere."

"Yes, very busy, yet never tiring."

We talked about the village she had come from and how she became a slave. At the end, having made a hat during this time, she gave it to me. It was a little large for my head, but nicely woven and of striking hues of red.

I talked to Selka many times, telling her about God's Son and the Virgin Mary. She listened, watching me as she wove, asking questions that I tried to answer in ways she would understand. Her questions were more to the point than those of Ceela Yaxche and she asked more of them. By the time winter arrived, I was certain that in her heart she had become a believer in the power of God, the message of Christ, and the mercy of the Virgin Mary.

I opened a second stall across the street, since I learned that Indians liked to compare prices. For a small sum I had the town rulers issue word that Selka and her mother were no longer *ppentacob,* and as free people could run the new store. They ran it well, indeed it soon rivaled mine.

I had a cross made for Selka, which she put up in the stall, and a string of wooden beads she hung about her neck. I could do no more. I was still a seminarian, with no power to bring her God's grace. Often I found myself wishing that the haughty, self-righteous Pedroza, who had refused my humble request, was sojourning in hell.

Early in the spring a Spanish ship came out of the north. I had time to warn the town rulers, who sent word through the streets. No one was to raise a hand against the Spaniards. They were to be given all the gold the Indians owned. And above all, told that to the south, six days' sailing, they would discover a city where the streets were paved with gold and people ate from gold plates. I warned Selka and her mother to stay indoors and attend to their weaving, making a grim joke that the Spaniards wore steel helmets and not straw hats.

For myself, I went into the jungle and stayed hidden for two weeks. When I came out the Spaniards had gone, leaving the town stripped of its gold and all of its fowl, but the Indians unharmed. There were many who were sorry to see them leave, so amazing were the animals that could carry a man and the armor that shone in the sun.

About two weeks later, people everywhere in the town began to have pains and grew so hot that their skins burned. Then red bumps appeared on their faces and bodies, and these became pustules. It was a terrible sickness and ran through the town like a brush fire, leaving people dead.

One morning Selka complained of a fever. By nightfall her honey-colored skin was blotched and red. Although I had heard of the disease in Spain — it was called *viruelas* — I had no idea of what to do.

Sola Mulamé went in search of a medicine man, but so great was the plague that four days passed before one came. He sat down beside Selka's bed and took a parcel of monkey fur, dried frogs, and moonstones from a pouch and spread them on the floor. Then he asked her to name the gods whom she thought might be molesting her. Was it Ah Muzen Cab, the bee god? Was it the long-nosed rain god, Chac? Was it Itzamná himself?

Selka turned her head and did not answer. The medicine man went away in disgust. I knelt beside the bed and held her hands and prayed, but I could do nothing to ease her pain. Because of the mulish Pedroza, who had sought out and courted martyrdom, I had never had the authority to baptize her. And now, as death stood by, I lacked the authority to speak of hope or comfort, not so much as a single word of the Christian rites.

She never took her gaze from me. It followed me about the room, and when I went out and came back it was still there, waiting to fix itself upon me again. Her face had become a hideous mask, but her eyes burned with the same trusting light. Her last words were, "Dear friend, please remember Selka in your prayers."

The incantations of witch doctors and the thousands of fervent pleas to Maya gods were in vain. In less than two months, half the people in Quintana were dead, hundreds were dying, and those who managed to recover, like the old woman and Selka's mother, rose from their beds with pocked and scarred faces. The incantations, however, were no more in vain than my Christian prayers.

I was saddened by Selka's death, but there was no time to mourn or even to worry about my own health. I left the stalls to the two women and joined the bands that collected the dead and built fires to consume them. The nights glowed with these lurid fires. The days were clouded by gray smoke.

The plague finally wore itself out and came to an end. Traders and merchants who had shunned Quintana during the sickness began to trickle back. Among them was a trader I had seen strolling through the marketplace followed by servants. I asked the old woman who he was.

"Zambac," she said, "or some name like that. He comes from a place to the south. In the mountains to the south."

"A man of importance?"

She shrugged. "He buys many things. And he has many porters to carry them away."

The trader's name was Zambac, Tzom Zambac, and he was one of the first traders I dealt with after the plague. He came in bouncing on his heels, the tassels on his sandals flapping merrily, and smiled and bowed twice before he was within speaking distance. He had two rolls of fat under his chin, two around his middle, and though he lacked one eye, had the jolliest face I have ever seen.

He bought a hat for each of his many servants and several for himself, not asking the price beforehand. All of this, however, was only a preliminary. He had come to talk business.

"I was here once before," he said, speaking a dialect I had never heard and found difficult. "I saw you as you sat on a blanket and sold trinkets like a common Indian. I was puzzled. I had met a band of your people when they traveled through my province. They were proud people who bought trinkets but did not sell them."

I was surprised to learn that the Spaniards had penetrated to the south of Quintana. "Did the white men come through the mountains or from the sea?"

"From the mountains. From Tenochtitlán. That is the city of the Aztéca."

"Was the leader called Cortés?"

"There was one they called *capitán*. Half the size of you, sir. He has a thin beard and thin hair. His face is very pale, like the bark of a ceiba. He limps along when he walks."

Surely Zambac was describing Cortés. Not Pedro de Alvarado nor Cristoval de Olid nor any of the other captains I knew.

"Does he have a woman with him?"

"Yes, a woman who speaks with many tongues. Marina, they call her."

Cortés, beyond doubt. Cortés!

"When he left your province, where did he go? In what direction?"

"He traveled . . . he traveled." Zambac paused to think. "He went southward. I remember now. Out of Maya country, along the Mumpango trail to the south."

Zambac frowned. He had not come to be questioned about matters he wasn't interested in.

"With your permission," he said, "I will talk about you." He waited for a moment and then bowed. "When I saw you squatting on a blanket I thought, There is a man who is white like this Cortés. But he is a poor seller of trinkets. A man of his size and whiteness, if he is a merchant in my country, would not be squatting in the sun like an Indian."

He paused to glance around at my open-air stall and its rows of sombreros. "You are standing now. Out of the rain and sun. But you are still poor. In my country you would someday be —" Zambac knew the Spanish word for 'rich person' — "a *rico*. But the two of us together would become big *ricos*. Not tomorrow, yet soon."

"You're a *rico* already."

"I wish to become more *rico*," he said. "Then I could buy a jewel like that one you wear on your finger. How many cacao do you wish for it, sir?"

"I do not wish to sell it," I said.

He moved closer. "I would like to put the ring on, sir, and see how beautiful it is on my finger."

"It's a *talismán*," I said. "A charm. An amulet. It is bad luck to take it off."

Not in the least offended by my refusal, he took a last admiring glance at the amethyst, gathered his servants, and backed away, his eyes on the floor. In the street, he bowed and called out in Spanish, "*Hasta luego*. Until then."

Tzom Zambac was at the stall when we opened, soon after daybreak. He came with ten porters and lined them up outside. Except for their hands and feet, they were barely visible under enormous bales of merchandise. He opened the top of one of the bales and pulled out a handful of red feathers.

"Toucan," he said and pointed to a second bale. "Yellow tanager. I also have hummingbird and five quetzals. Others also."

He sent the porters away. Swaying under their light but cumbersome burdens, led by guards and servants, they disappeared along the road that followed the more southerly of the two rivers. He turned to me and bowed.

"I can see that you have thought much since I was here," he said.

"I haven't thought at all. You talked about my being your partner. Partner in what?"

"On the Isle of Petén, where I live, you will be a partner in the selling of feathered cloaks. I have them made with the feathers you have seen. Beautiful cloaks. You go about and sell the cloaks to nobles."

"Go about? Where? What nobles?"

"You go about to towns near Petén. There are many nobles in these towns. Many. They will see that you are a noble too, a noble white man, and they will buy cloaks . . ."

"And pay more for them than usual."

Tzom Zambac lightly touched my arm to assure me that this was exactly what he had in mind.

"Two times as much. Three times. Perhaps four times," he said. "Because a white man, a noble white man like you, sir, brings good fortune to everything that he touches with his hands. The white man has powerful spirits around him. You can see them at night. They glow in the darkness around his body."

"Did the man Cortés glow in the dark?"

"Like a jewel. Like a necklace of jewels," Tzom Zambac said. "I will give you a part of what you sell, white noble." He glanced at the jewel, the beautiful amethyst ring on my finger.

"What part?" I asked.

"After the costs, one half."

I was not overwhelmed by the prospect of selling feathered cloaks to the nobles of Petén. But any day, at any hour, Cortés might appear in Quintana. I couldn't hide, as I had hidden in Chichén-Palapa, where everyone was my friend. Here, if Cortés were to offer an inducement in the form of gold, or a bout of Spanish torture such as hanging upside down, someone would surely betray me.

Above all, I was haunted by memories of Selka Mulamé. During the days, and at night in my dreams, I saw her gaze fixed upon me. I often heard the last trusting words she had spoken — "Dear friend, please remember Selka in your prayers." Quintana was a dead place to me.

We left it the next morning. I turned over the stalls to the women to run as they saw fit until I returned, which would be never. I took little — my pearls, a pouch of cacao beans and triangular bits of copper to serve as money, and the wide-brimmed hat that Selka had made.

I left in the same spiritless mood that I had when I left the cove and Chichén-Palapa, without the least idea of what lay before me and not much caring — a godless wanderer, seeking nothing. Deep down in my thoughts was the dire warning from Leviticus, "And ye shall flee when none pursueth you."

We overtook the porters that night at a hostel of thatch and saplings open on all sides, owned by an elderly Indian who called it Ix Ykoki, or Evening Star, after his granddaughter. Zambac and I were given hot water for baths and fish for supper that tasted like pork. The granddaughter, who ran from chore to chore and hummed plaintive little tunes under her breath, reminded me of Selka.

We never found such a commodious hostel again, although there were many places along the trail, located a comfortable day's travel apart, where we could buy fire for our evening meal and fresh meat, usually tapir or opossum, occasionally dog, which the porters preferred.

We alternately baked and froze as our train climbed out of the hotlands into the high mountain passes and down through ravines that crisscrossed each other and still ran bank to bank with water from the rains. At all the crossings there were hanging bridges woven of vines that swayed and creaked over the rushing torrents. Zambac was now riding in a litter. Every step I took over the rough trail, I longed for the stallion Bravo.

My new partner was the politest man I had ever known. He greeted everyone we passed on the trail, displaying his open palms in the Maya greeting. On the other hand, he was the most suspicious. Everyone we encountered, whether a lone traveler, traders with a dozen porters, or a cacique accompanied by a horde of slaves, guards, and women, he sized up as potential brigands out to do him in.

Our line of porters and servants and guards wound toward the Isle of Petén at a snake's pace, scarcely five leagues each day, stopping often to rest those who carried Zambac. As the sun set I sang Ave Maria, surprised to learn that during the time Cortés had spent among them everyone had come to enjoy it. But at dawn they all plucked thorns and greeted the rising sun, I among them.

The lake of Petén was hidden by a blue mist when we came to its shores early in the morning after ten days of hard travel from Quintana. The city of Petén was located on an island in the middle of the lake, so our caravan had to wait until the mist lifted and canoes were able to ferry us across.

I had been told by Zambac that it was the most beautiful of all the Maya cities, but had put no trust in his words, attributing them to his tendency to boast. I was wrong. When the mist lifted, the sun revealed rows of glittering temples that reached into the sky.

Noting my astonishment, Zambac said, "Petén was more beautiful before this man Cortés came. Cortés burned the god-houses. Cortés tore down our stone idols. Cortés took the stones and did bad things with them."

I remembered that I had been equally dazzled by my first view of the City of the Seven Serpents. I likewise remembered my disappointment when I entered the city and found it a collection of ruins. These memories sobered me as I stood there on the shore gazing across the waters at the shining towers.

I was surprised, therefore, when we crossed to the island and came upon the central plaza. Petén was, indeed, a beautiful city.

On two sides of the plaza and raised from the level where people walked were stone structures of varying heights painted in raw shades of blue and yellow and red. Facing each other were the temples I had viewed from the shore, towering stark white and, like those I had seen in Tenochtitlán, washed with glistening mica. Broad streets that rayed out from the plaza like spokes in a wheel were planted with flowers, and flowering vines trailed down from the rooftops. There were crosses everywhere.

My eye was caught by a gigantic statue of red sandstone that rose from the center of the plaza. It was roughly hewn but unmistakably the figure of a riderless horse, with flowing tail and two hooves pawing the air. According to Zambac, it was the pride of Petén and all the countryside.

"Cortés," he said, "rode into the city on the back of a red animal. The beast had a bad injury in its foot, and when Cortés went away, he left the horse behind him. My people loved the beast. They offered it flowers to eat and fruit and savory stews of dog and turkey to cure its bad foot, but the animal grew pale and died. So the people made a statue of the beast. Now they worship it as the god of thunder and lightning. What do you believe, sir? Do you believe that it has the power of a god?"

"If the people believe it does, then it does."

"What do you believe, sir?"

"I say that it has power."

"What would Cortés say if he returned? He burned all the idols and warned the people not to worship anyone except the God in heaven."

People were bringing flowers, lying prone before the effigy while we talked.

"What would this man say if he returned, sir?"

"He would say nothing, Zambac. He would shake his head, fall to his knees in prayer, then get up and burn the city to the ground and put a thousand to the sword."

"The statue?"

"He would break it into small pieces and throw it in the lake."

"Do you feel like doing the same, sir?"

"No," I said. "Not at all."

Zambac smiled and rubbed his palms. "I see that you will do well with our nobles. They will like you, sir, and you will sell many cloaks at excellent prices. We will become *ricos* very soon, sir."

Zambac was a prophet, as well as a good businessman. Before a month had passed, I sold fifteen hummingbird cloaks without leaving the city and took orders for nine more at triple the prices commanded in the past. The cloaks were works of art, like those made in Zambac's shops long before I came. But the fear in which all Spaniards were held, the reverence they inspired, the awe caused by my blond hair and great height — I was two heads taller than Cortés — and above all the belief in the mysterious powers of the white man, made it possible for me to meet the noblest of the nobles, the important *batak,* who collected taxes, the high priest, the *nacom,* and the leader, the *halach uinic* himself.

Zambac's enterprise, located in an alley near the central plaza, consisted of a series of small rooms surrounded by a courtyard planted with flowering jacaranda trees. In each room there were three women. They chose the designs and sketched them on the best cotton cloth stretched drumhead tight over hardwood panels. They could show any of a dozen different pastoral scenes, such as deer grazing beside a mountain brook, or a martial scene of warriors with banners flying under a canopy of stars and clouds.

The design was important. Much time was spent patiently listening to customers who wanted a scene they had devised themselves. But in the end, whatever the design, it was the workmanship that counted. Zambac was an artist and he hired only artists. The women were more skilled than the best goldsmiths. They were like fine painters who used feathers instead of pigments to create their masterpieces.

Zambac allowed neither short cuts nor cheating. In a cloak that had six thousand feathers, none larger than a frond of maidenhair fern, some as small as a mayfly's wing, not so much as one feather was tinted to suit the color desired. Not one was trimmed to fit a certain space. The *goma* that fastened the feathers to the cotton backing was transparent, faintly and pleasingly aromatic.

I was enthralled by the beauty of these shimmering cloaks. I had no twinge of conscience when I demanded and received triple the price they once had sold for. At that, considering the mysterious powers I added to the transaction as a white man, the nobles got a bargain.

The artists couldn't keep up with the orders I brought in. We ran out of feathers, and Zambac went off with a caravan of fleet-footed porters to purchase more. The porters returned before he did, with news that the warrior, the one who had visited Petén and left his lame animal, had sailed into and out of the harbor while they were in Quintana. To my questions they replied that he had sailed northward, his men saying that they were on their way to Vera Cruz and Tenochtitlán. It was welcome news. At last I could put Hernán Cortés behind me. At last!

Zambac returned soon afterward, accompanied by two dozen Quintana porters loaded down with more feathers. He was in high spirits and full of new plans.

"There was Zambac," Zambac said, thumping himself on the chest. "There he was looking at the most wonderful feathers ever seen — macaw, tanager, hummingbirds blessed by tails three feet in length, doves, crested parrots, seven egrets, seven quetzals of a beauty never surpassed. And cheap. Cheap, sir! Then Zambac remembered . . ."

He was speaking of himself as someone else, as a third person, to lessen the effect upon me of bad news, I presumed.

"Then Zambac remembered that he had not shared our profits since the day the business began. And he said to himself, this must be talked about the day he returns to Petén. The hour, perhaps."

"So you bought the beautiful feathers," I said, amused.

I was in no need of money — I never got used to thinking of cacao beans and snippets of tin as money. I lived comfortably in a lean-to located at the back of the courtyard. I ate my meals with Zambac and usually overate — he could consume a small turkey without help. At dawn I walked out to the plaza, where people were on their knees praying before the stone horse, waiting for sunrise. Sometimes I joined them in their rites to the sun. This period, I think, was the happiest of my life in the land of the Maya. I had nothing. I wanted nothing.

"And, sir, we will dispose of them at beautiful prices," Zambac was saying. "In places you have not been ever. Like Tikal. Like Copán. Even as far as Coclé. And the places on the sea — Homoc-nac-kaknab, where the sea boils yellow."

We were forced to buy a room across the way to store our feathers and hire another artist to fashion them into cloaks. We branched out into headdresses, which proved to be more profitable than the cloaks, since they required less work. With two items to sell and our customers at a distance of a day or more from Petén, I was on the trail much of the time.

Before the summer rains began, I journeyed to Tikal, three days' hard travel to the south. Tikal — from what I had seen and heard from travelers — had been the largest of the Maya cities, reaching out for a dozen leagues in all directions.

It was now mostly a jumble of mounds and ruins, like the City of the Seven Serpents. But in a vast central plaza, situated between two towering heaps of stone that had once been temples, people from the surrounding jungle met to sell things and to worship before an effigy of coiled snakes.

The bustling settlement had a horde of black-robed priests,

as blood-caked as those in the City of the Seven Serpents, many lords, and a powerful cacique, Ah Machika. On the morning I arrived in Tikal I saw him striding through the plaza in a feathered robe and plumed jaguar mask, a stiff, impressive figure attended by a retinue of slaves and guards. I met him soon afterward as he sat on a stone slab in one of the ruined buildings, holding court among a crowd of petitioners and wrongdoers.

My turn to be heard came last, just after Ah Machika had banished a young man from the settlement for stealing a bowl of corncakes and sentenced a woman to have her hair shorn off for meeting the eye of a traveler, a stranger she had not seen before.

Others had approached him on their knees, and I did the same. But before I had crawled halfway toward him, he motioned me to stand. He removed his mask, revealing a typical Maya head — a long, heavy beak of a nose thrusting out from a slanted brow, the result of having it squeezed between boards as an infant. But his eyes, instead of being crossed in the fashionable mode, stared straight at me, little pieces of obsidian black as night and cold.

"I have heard words about you," he said in a rumbling voice that befit his size. "You are here to sell me something I do not want."

"No, I have come because I have heard of you, as you have heard of me, honorable cacique. To see for myself the man who is known everywhere, as far away as the Isle of Petén, for his kindness and generosity and a mind sharp like a serpent's tooth."

I had heard these same compliments when I was Kukulcán. I had spoken them in Tenochtitlán to the emperor Moctezuma. They had impressed me and also Moctezuma, but they did not impress Ah Machika. He stared at me with his black eyes.

"I had news from people that you were tall," he said, "and

I saw a tall man in my thoughts. But you are taller than a man. You are tall like a tree."

I had a suspicion that the cacique considered me a freak, as others had before him, and that as such I was about to be offered inducements to remain in the village of Tikal. My suspicion was partly correct. Before I left the next day, with an order for two hummingbird cloaks trimmed in the silky fur of araguatos, red-bearded howling monkeys, the cacique in an elaborate ceremony made me a lord of the realm and promised me fabulous gifts should I return.

"This city is where the gods have stored their gold. Only here in Tikal," he said. "You are a white man, and you will know what to say to the white men when they come here and ask for gold. As they have done elsewhere."

"You know about the white men?"

"I have heard."

"About Quintana?"

"Yes."

"About Cortés, who came to Petén and burned the temples?"

"Yes, about Cortés," the cacique said. "About him I have heard much."

Near the end of summer, when our store of feathers began to run low, Zambac departed for Quintana. After he had been gone for several weeks, a runner brought word from him that he had found the warehouses bare — the few feathers to be had were of an inferior quality, mostly from small, dull-colored parrots.

During the summer, in the jungles north and south of Panamá, there had been a series of fierce hurricanes, each more devastating than the one before. Fruit trees had been leveled. Insects swept away. Flowering bushes ripped from the earth. Struck down by the horrendous winds or starved by lack of food, birds perished by the millions. A meadow had been seen where a flock of hummingbirds lay in a gray carpet, rotting in the sun.

One bright morning, a few days after the runner appeared, Zambac returned empty-handed except for one small, pathetic bundle of parrot feathers. But to my amazement, after he had washed off the grime of a week's journey and slept soundly through the afternoon, he came to the supper table that night showing no signs of disappointment. He sat down and took up his knife, cut a slab of iguana, which he doused on all sides in a pyramid of salt, maneuvered the meat into his mouth, and thoughtfully began to chew, meanwhile smiling at me across the table.

Zambac was a happy man — he even woke up in the morning with a smile. As the day progressed, the smile broadened, but on this night it seemed broader than usual.

"We cannot make feathered cloaks without feathers," I said. "And it will be a long time before we can buy more."

Zambac counted out the twenty days of the Maya month from Imix to Ahau. Then he added up the months until he came to a *tun,* 360 days. Then he doubled the *tun* and held up two fingers, which brought the total to 720 days in Spanish numbers.

"A long time," I said.

"Long," he said, and called to a servant to bring him more salt. "Long."

"Long enough to starve," I said.

He nodded, cut himself a second slab of meat, and went through his ritual of dousing it with the salt the servant brought. Torchlight shone on his forehead, which now began to show a fine coating of sweat.

"What plans for not starving did you bring back from Quintana?" I asked him.

"I have many plans from Quintana," he said between chews. "But only one shines out like a bright star in the sky."

He finished his mouthful and took a draught of mild *balche* wine. Then he sat back and fixed his one good eye on my amethyst ring, glowing like a crystal flower in the light from the torches.

"It is very difficult, this plan. It has more points than ten porcupines," he said. "You can get yourself stung with this plan. Both of us, but you mostly."

He rinsed his mouth with *balche* and spat it out. He glanced at the iguana briefly, then his eye again fixed itself on the amethyst. During the time I had lived in Petén not a day had passed without some mention of the ring — its beauty, how it came into my possession, its worth, on and on. He was obsessed with the amethyst ring.

"Down below in Quintana," he said, "the first day I was

walking in the market looking for feathers — the two women do well in your stalls making hats, by the way — on that first day in the morning this white man who came here to Petén and left his animal that they made a statue of . . ."

"Cortés."

"Cortés, yes. This man was walking in the market also, and he came up to me and said that he remembered when he was up in Petén that he got a cloak from me. I think it was the eye he remembered . . . He said he bought a cloak from me — he bought a cloak, that is true, but did not pay . . . Anyhow, he wished to know if I had ever seen a tall man, a very tall white man, or heard of such a tall white man . . ."

Zambac squirmed out of his jacket and tossed it away. The night was very hot. Bats were swooping about, chasing insects in the jacaranda bushes. Insects were flying into the torches, making little frying sounds as the flames consumed them. Zambac pushed the iguana aside and put his bare elbows on the table and called for a fan.

I waited for him to continue. Usually he spoke rapidly, biting off the ends of his words. Tonight they were oozing out of his mouth. He had something to tell me, but didn't know how to go about it.

"And of course," I said, "being my friend, you waited until you knew exactly why Cortés was asking about me. You didn't say right off that you had seen a tall white man roaming around in the streets of Petén. That . . ."

"Oh, no, sir," Zambac said. "Oh, no, sir."

"What did you say?"

"I said . . ." Zambac paused. "I did not answer Cortés at once. I wrinkled my forehead and thought. Then something came to me right out of the sky . . ."

He glanced up at the dark sky novering above the light from the torches, as if he expected something more to come tumbling down to him.

" 'I have not seen this tall white man,' I said to Cortés. 'But I have heard that others have seen him. Not in Petén. In places farther to the south.' Cortés said, 'In Tikal?' And I said, 'Yes, in Tikal.' Then this Cortés went away, but the next morning he came up and asked if I could find you. If I could find you and bring back . . . not you exactly, but something. Your hand that has the ring on it."

"My hand would show that you had found me?"

"Yes, sir."

"What was his offer for this small service?"

"Big," Zambac said, making a sweeping gesture that took in the world. "I will be the cacique of all Quintana. Of Petén likewise."

"You *will* be or you *would* be?" I asked.

The distinction between the two was lost on Zambac, and I had to repeat the question in different words.

He laughed, took a hearty drink of *balche,* and said, "I asked him, this Cortés, if he would be pleased with the ring only. He shook his head. I said I would bring a finger. But he shook his head again. He wished everything — the ring and the hand both."

"Where is Cortés now?"

"Going to Tenochtitlán."

"If he is going to Tenochtitlán, how can you give him my hand?"

"He has fast runners down there in Quintana waiting now."

"And when they get the hand they will run fast to Tenochtitlán and give it to Cortés," I said, half-amused at the whole idea.

Zambac had quit smiling and was slowly getting himself drunk.

"How do you become the cacique of Quintana and also Petén if Cortés is up in Tenochtitlán? Did he tell you that?"

"Yes, he told me. In Quintana there is a white captain now

and his men. Twenty men. Cortés left them when he went away, and they rule Quintana. Cortés took me by the arm to this captain and gave him a command to make me the cacique of Quintana and likewise Petén when I was finished with things."

The servant was standing behind him, waving a big palmetto fan. Zambac wore his hair in a bang and the breeze from the fan kept moving it up and down.

"Alala," Zambac burst out. "This is what came out of the sky."

He glanced up at the sky once more and then down at the ring. I moved my hand out of sight.

"It came to me," he said, for some reason lowering his voice, "that you will give me the ring. Take it off and give it to Zambac. Then Zambac will search around and find a hand somewhere and put the ring on it . . . You see what came out of the sky?"

"The hand you search for, Zambac, and find hereabouts will be the hand of an Indian. Not the hand of a white man."

"I have thought about this, sir. This will not be hard for Zambac. He will change the hand from brown to white by the milk of a ficus tree. Then he will dry the hand in the sun. Perhaps he will put a white man's tattoo on it. How would a cross be, like the crosses this Cortés left around everywhere in Petén?"

"The cross is an inspired thought," I said. "Did it also come from the sky?"

"From the sky," Zambac said, pointed overhead, and ordered a second gourd of *balche* and another fan. "Down from the sky, sir."

A breeze drifted through the courtyard, but it was still hot. The fans kept moving up and down after Zambac went to sleep. I had the servants put him to bed in the hammock that swung between two jacaranda trees. I waited until they left, then I tied up his hands and feet with cords I cut from the hammock.

I had nothing much to take. The streets were deserted, except for a homeless dog that followed me to the plaza. There he sniffed about and finally lifted his leg on the statue of Cortés' horse and left. A small moon was riding along in a cloudless sky. By its light I found a canoe and paddled across the lake. I walked until dawn on the trail that led to Tikal, then slept for a while, then went on at a rapid gait.

I stayed in the ruined city of Tikal through the next summer and another winter. I lived in a wing of a palace that was quite similar to my palace in the City of the Seven Serpents, even to its broken statues, stained walls, and vermin.

Ah Machika had his quarters in another wing of the six wings that formed the huge, star-shaped structure. After a week or so, when he made no mention of the gold he had told me about in such glowing terms, I brought up the subject one night at supper. I had come to Tikal to evade Zambac, true enough, but I had not forgotten the promise my host had made.

Ah Machika was apologetic. "I forget," he said. "I am old and forgetful. Tomorrow, soon, we go and you will see that what I told you is correct."

We didn't go on the next day or soon, though I mentioned the gold every few nights at dinner. I came to the belief that he was deliberately delaying the matter, fearful that if once I got my hands on the treasure I would take what I could carry and then disappear. It was also possible that the treasure did not exist. He valued the impression that I made on his subjects and the travelers who came by — there were many, since the town was not only on a main trade route but also at the gateway of the trail that led to Mount Chicanel, the Concealer, home of Tzelta, the sibyl.

In the distant past Tikal had been a flourishing trade center, larger than Quintana, situated as it was on the east-west trails between the Southern Ocean and the Sea of Caribs and other trails connecting it to Tenochtitlán in the far north. It had also been a great religious center, drawing hordes of Maya worshippers. Now the trails were heavily used by commercial traders and known to the Spaniards.

Spaniards came in bands, mostly on horses, and well armed with muskets or harquebuses, even with small cannon pulled by mules. At first they were apt to be respectful of Ah Machika's army, for the soldiers with their crossed eyes and naked bodies coated with soot were fearsome to behold. But they never left without causing trouble. One band, told that there was no gold to be had, set up cannon and fired at the palace.

Ah Machika, who had never heard a cannon or seen an iron ball as big as his head flying through the air, fell on his knees and begged forgiveness for his poverty. I prevailed upon him to hold fast and not to tell them about the gold, that they would soon run out of powder, which they did. Whereupon he seized the Spaniards, arranged a feast day, and sacrificed them one by one to the hungry sun god.

There were mounds in Tikal ten times the number found on my island. They extended in a line more than a league wide and for twenty leagues, in what appeared to be a series of plazas faced by temples, government structures, and the abodes of the city's nobles — all devoured by vines and creepers, sunk beneath a quiet verdant sea, marked only by trees that grew from the rooftops.

I did no exploring. I was not tempted to restore any of the buildings near the palace in which I lived. And if I had undertaken such a rash task, it would have failed.

The people of Tikal — some two thousand were left of what must have been, judging from the vast numbers of mounds, a city of a hundred thousand — were content to farm their small *milpas,* eat corncakes and red beans at every meal, drink copious amounts of *balche,* congregate on feast days, and have many children, of whom more than half died before they were a year old. Like the people of my lost island.

However, while I waited upon Ah Machika and his gold, growing more suspicious that he was gulling me, more restless day by day, from time to time weighing the advantages of throwing in my lot with one of the Spanish bands, of forcing Ah Machika to act, of even wringing the truth from him, if necessary, I had hours to spare. I spent them in an attempt to decipher the Maya past.

There were no books in the palace, such as those I had studied in the City of the Seven Serpents. I had to be content with the stelae scattered about in the plaza. Most were in good condition, but most of their glyphs dealt with dates — who ruled the city in a certain year, the length of his rule, and nothing else. There was no clue, no more than in the books I had studied before, to the great mystery.

The Persian empire had disappeared, as had the Assyrian empire, and those of the Egyptians, the Greeks, and the Romans, but not overnight. Why, in the matter of a few brief years, had the Maya suddenly stopped building their magnificent temples? Why had they quit constructing splendid causeways, buttressed with cut stone, that led to the temples? Why had they deserted their palaces and elaborate edifices to disappear into the jungle — as if the voices of the gods and of the stars they worshipped, speaking as one single voice, had commanded them to cease doing what they had done for a thousand years. Or was it that they heard no voice, no command, that they had suddenly lost faith in the gods and the stars?

There was no sign here in Tikal, as there had been none on the Island of the Seven Serpents, in Chichén-Palapa, Quintana, or Petén, that earthquakes or famine or disease had weakened the Maya will to carry on the traditions that they had inherited. But there were signs, the same ones I had seen before, that the reasons for the cataclysm might lie with the priesthood. As elsewhere, the Tikal priests went about in dirty gowns, their long hair caked with filth — thin, dark figures who camped in the ruins and made predictions that didn't come true as often as they did.

We had a steady stream of these dolorous apparitions coming from all directions, pausing for a night or two and moving on. During my first month in Tikal, two of them arrived by the north trail who looked to be twin brothers. They were a pair whom I felt I had seen before, possibly in Quintana. I had seen them, true enough, but not in Quintana. They came from the Isle of Petén, sent hither by Zambac.

I was awakened toward morning of a stormy night by a scuttling sound. I slept on a pallet near a window — one without glass, like all Maya windows — and thought it was a coatimundi, a snake, an iguana, or some other of the small animals that paid me nocturnal visits. I thought this until I felt a sharp pain at my wrist, something tugging at my finger, and caught the fetid breath of an assailant groping for my throat.

I lunged from my pallet, taking my attacker, who by now had a good hold on my neck, with me. His feet were dangling from the floor as I walked to the window and tossed him out. The second assailant had already fled. At dawn, as soon as he heard my story, Ah Machika dispatched a band of fast runners and captured the pair. He sacrificed them weeks later to the spring god, Xipe Totec, and sent a severed finger from each to Zambac in Petén.

Many months after this incident, when Ah Machika judged that I was getting ready to leave Tikal, he took me to the gold fields. Carried in litters, we traveled for hours until we reached a broad river. On both sides of the river were vast stretches of what appeared to be golden sand.

"There," the cacique said, extending his arms in a kingly gesture. "Feast your eyes!"

The sun was overhead, pouring down upon fields of shining

gold, windrows and swales and dunes of gold. There were no trails leading in or out of the glittering expanse. No sign of human tracks, though I did make out just beyond me the delicate marks of a lizard's claws.

The scene blinded my eyes. It could not be. It was impossible that so much gold could exist in the world.

And it *was* impossible. I had taken no more than a step when I realized that I was treading upon thin, dustlike particles — not like those I had seen in the riverbed on Isla del Oro. It was not gold that lay before me, shimmering in the sun, but worthless pyrites — fool's gold.

I concealed my disappointment as best I could. "Wonderful," I said, clapping my hands together like a child. "The gods have been kind to you."

"To us," the cacique said. "We share the gods' treasure. The two of us."

I wondered if he was being honest with me, if he really believed that the worthless stuff was gold. "You have never used it?" I asked him. "Made ornaments — beads or rings, anything at all?"

"Tzelta the sibyl forbade me," he said. "Long ago now she spoke a warning not to touch the gold. Not to come near that gold until the day."

"What day?"

"The day a white cloud from the sky came down and walked like a man . . ."

"I am the cloud?"

"You are the white cloud that walks," Ah Machika said firmly, as though he believed it. "We share the gold, yes?"

"We'll melt it into bars," I said. "Beautiful gold bars."

"What will be done then?"

"We'll make ornaments of the bars. Rings. Necklaces. Gold plates to eat from."

The cacique's black eyes danced.

I left Tikal early the next morning, promising him to return in a few days to help collect our gold. I harbored no ill will toward Ah Machika. I was only angry at myself for wasting months, a year, almost two years on the wildest of chases.

I took the south trail from Tikal, since the north trail would have led me back toward Petén. It was well traveled on this morning. Caravans were moving both ways, from as far north as Tenochtitlán and from distant places to the south.

Late that afternoon I came to a fork in the trail, where several Indian caravans were encamped. Upon inquiring, I learned that the left fork led to Panamá. Further inquiry disclosed that the right fork led to the cave of the sibyl Tzelta, and that all in the encampment had visited her that day.

A small island to the north of the Island of the Seven Serpents housed a sibyl who counseled women who were either pregnant or wished to be. Married or unmarried, young or old, they poured in upon her from the mainland, from everywhere.

I had never had an occasion to visit this sibyl, but I was acquainted with her reputation for prophecy and miracles. I recalled that Ah Machika had visited the sibyl Tzelta. Although I was not impressed with the advice she had given him, in a bitter mood, still blaming myself for time wasted, I decided to take the fork that led to her cave.

I arrived there at dusk to find a dozen or more supplicants waiting to see her. The sessions went on through the night and through the next day. At dawn of the second day, I was led by two masked women dressed in yellow, diaphanous robes into an opening, no more than a crevice, in the face of a wooded mountain.

I was escorted down a passageway, at the end of which was a row of candles set into a wall. Below the candles, which gave off a curious scent, was an even narrower passage, one that required me to get down on my hands and knees.

The women left me, with instructions to crawl forward until

I came to a room lit by only one candle. Here I was to lie prone, put my ear to the floor, and listen. I was not to ask questions. Questions resulted in misunderstanding. They led nowhere. They would not be answered. I was to give only my name and destination.

Crawling forward into a dark room not much larger than a closet, lit by one small candle set in the mouth of a grinning serpent, I lay flat on the stone floor and listened. At first all I heard was a buzzing in my ears, caused by exertion. Then my ears cleared and I heard the rapid beating of my heart. The beating grew faint and suddenly was enveloped in deep silence.

"My name is Julián Escobar," I said, as I had been instructed.

There was no answer, only the distant sound of my words and silence again. I remembered that I had been told to give my destination. I had none. The silence deepened. Then I remembered that I had been told that one of the forks in the trail led to a place called Panamá. I said the strange name in a shaking voice.

From far below me the name was repeated. It sounded like an echo of my own voice, yet it was the voice of a girl, someone very young and far away. I waited, scarcely taking a breath.

"That land where the great seas meet," the sibyl intoned. She spoke softly, in Maya but with the accent of an Aztecatl. "What is it you seek in this place?"

I was silent, making certain that I answered her truthfully. I was not there in a musty cell, lying on a wet, hard stone, to give foolish answers.

"You are silent. You hesitate and chew your thumb, not knowing why you go to Panamá?"

She no longer sounded like a sibyl but like a woman who, having encountered many Spaniards, was on the verge of anger.

"Being a Spaniard," she said, "you will know that you go for one reason. Spaniards search for one thing. Not for love. Not for friends. Not for land. Not to plant crops and harvest them. They search only for gold and nothing else."

"For gold, nothing else." Then, forgetting that I was not to ask questions, I said, "Where can it be found?"

There was a long silence. I feared that I had incurred her wrath.

"Not in Panamá," she finally answered. "South from Panamá, in another place, there's a man who is called Inca. Each morning this lord is carried to a sacred lake. He takes off his night clothing and priests cover him with sweet oils. Then he is covered with gold dust, even his face and private possessions. Then, as dawn breaks, he walks into the lake and washes himself. Every day of the year he does this, except when he is on journeys. His father did this and his grandfather also. At the bottom of the lake gold lies thick."

I had heard this tale on the deck of the *Santa Margarita* from one of the crew, long before I reached New Spain. It meant nothing to me then. It did now.

"But first you must find the place where the two great seas meet," the sibyl continued, "and the man in a flame-colored doublet."

"A Spaniard?"

"In a flame-colored doublet, who walks with a slight limp."

"There are many such. What is his name?"

"His name escapes me. It has a meaning, however, like Uitzilopochtli. But it is not that, not Witchy Wolves. In a week, in six days, I will remember."

"Only one man knows about the gold? A man in a red doublet?"

There was no answer. I asked the question again. Still there was no answer. I pressed my ear hard against the stone. I heard nothing but primordial silence, so deep that it sounded like a river rushing leagues below me under the mountain. I began to shiver from the cold. Scrambling to my knees, I crawled back through the passage, into the sunlight at last, and took the trail that led to the south, in search of a man in a red doublet.

A fierce storm had blown up, but I did not pause. The words of the seeress were burned into my flesh.

•
•

I found the man who wore a flame-colored doublet and walked with a slight limp on my first day in the Spanish town of Panamá. Indeed, as I came out of the jungle after four hellish weeks on the trail south from the cave of the Maya sibyl, he crossed the street at a distance from me, a small figure in a wide-brimmed hat pulled down over his eyes against the noontime glare. Had I not stepped behind a tree and waited until he passed out of sight, we would have met there on the street.

I had two reasons for evading him at that moment. Stripped down to skin and bones from weeks of hard travel, my face swollen by insect bites, my lips cracked from the tropical sun, I was a poor specimen to ask a favor of anyone. Furthermore, since I had heard on the way that the town was populated by Spaniards lately come from Spain, there was a good chance that this man in the red doublet had learned from someone that I was being sought by Cortés and the Governor of Hispaniola.

I slept the rest of the day at a hovel calling itself the Inn of the Virgin, burned my Maya rags, and bought Spanish clothes with the next to last pearl I owned. That night, after a heavy rain, I ventured into streets that lay knee-deep in mud and visited a dive where I would run no risk of meeting the man in the red doublet. La Perla, the Pearl, a corral that stabled horses and had a long trestle on one side, served *balche* in earthen cups.

I learned that the man I sought was named Francisco Pizarro, that everyone in Panamá knew Pizarro, that half the inhabitants hated Pizarro, the rest loved him, and with both he was feared as a man of dangerous pride, soft-hearted at moments, tough as Toledo steel, and always unpredictable.

A leathery young soldier — one dressed in quilted armor, at least, whose skin had been scorched by many suns — bought me a cup of *balche*. I thought I had seen him before in Tenochtitlán, but this proved to be wrong. He had never been north of Panamá and had never heard of Hernán Cortés.

He said, throwing an arm around my shoulder, "When you came through the door, *amigo,* it gave me a start. I thought to myself, A tree, Sainted Mother, and it walks. It walks like a man."

From this Tomás Calderón I learned much more than if I had gone straight to Francisco Pizarro and said, "General, I would like to hear about the gold that exists there in the land of the Inca Indians, which everyone speaks about and with which you are familiar, having been in this land."

"The country," Tomás said, "is vast beyond the telling. Mountains — they must touch the moon — rear themselves high in the east. To the west the sea surges for hundreds of leagues. Between them lies the rich country of the Inca. The nobles eat with gold knives from gold plates. They tread streets paved with gold. They wear gold sandals with gold tassels, and great gold loops hang from their ears."

I asked about the prince who covered himself with gold each morning and bathed himself in a sacred lake, the one the sibyl had described.

"Yes, I have heard of this," he said. "His name is Atahualpa. His people call him Lupe Luzir, King of Great Kings, Child of the Sun, Inca."

"If all that gold lies there, why is Pizarro here?" I asked.

Tomás Calderón, though a young man, carried the signs of

a veteran. Both cheeks bore scars, and his long nose, which he kept rubbing with one hand as he drank, had been broken in recent days.

"Pizarro's here because he is just returned from Spain. He has enemies, you know, dozens. He went to Spain to confound them by getting the king's blessing for his enterprises. And by God's mercy, he got it. Now he's governor and captain-general of all of New Castile. Not of the country that lies north of here. That country's smaller, half the size of New Castile. Has a different governor."

"Who?" I asked, though I knew it to be Hernán Cortés.

Tomás shrugged and drank down the cup of *balche* he had been holding. Then he drew out his sword, waved it above his head, and charged at a group of Indians at the far end of the trestle, shouting, *"Vayan diablos morenos,* out, brown devils. *Vayan!"*

I slipped away during the melee that followed, but the next night, having remained hidden all day, I learned at the same tavern all that I needed to know about Francisco Pizarro. My informant was a young Indian named Felipillo, Little Philip, who introduced himself as an interpreter for Pizarro. I asked him if the general was acquainted with Hernán Cortés.

He snickered, showing small white teeth sharp as a ferret's. "His mother is related by blood to Cortés. Governor-General Pizarro has been in the New World for many years. He's acquainted with everyone. He was at Balboa's side when that explorer discovered the ocean we can see here now, pounding on the beach out there in the dark. He has known Cortés for a long time. They are friends, these men."

"When did they last see each other?"

"I have been with Governor-General Pizarro for six years. And in that time the two have not met."

"Or exchanged letters?"

"Letters? Ha. Where do you think you are, in Seville?" He

squinted his eyes and gave me a quick look. "You ask a lot of questions, señor," he added as he left, a fine sword, which was nearly as long as he was tall, clanking at his heels.

I lay down on my flea-infested bed that night, easy in my mind for the first time since my arrival in Panamá, certain that Pizarro had heard nothing about me from Cortés.

The next morning I went in search of the governor-general. I found him on the beach in the midst of a gang of workers loading the longboat of a ship anchored close offshore. Except for his red doublet, I would not have picked him out of the crowd. He was diminutive, even among the small Spanish workmen who surrounded him.

Catching sight of me from the corner of his eye, he turned his back and kept me waiting until the longboat was loaded, went on its way, and reached the caravel. Only then did he turn to stare.

"Your honor," I said, holding my ground, deciding it would be better than if I approached him. "I have heard that you are looking for men."

"Not looking," he said.

It was a rebuff, delivered in a gravelly voice.

"Who are you?" he said, continuing to stare.

"Julián Escobar," I said.

"From whence?"

"From Maya country. Near that of the Aztéca."

"Then you have encountered my friend Hernán Cortés."

"Many times, sir."

"A fine man. But overly ambitious. He ranges far. Too far."

Pizarro walked to where I stood and looked up at me. It was done simply and without swagger, yet the effect was one of defiance, saying to me, "Young man, you are in the presence of the Governor-General of New Castile, take off your hat."

I did so.

"We can use a man of your dimensions," he said. "What do you do well? Set sails without climbing a ladder?"

"I have been a steersman."

"On land, what can you do?"

"I am a good walker, sir. I have just walked here from five hundred leagues away and more."

"A recommendation," Pizarro said. "There is much walking to be done once we reach land. Through country wilder than the configurations of hell. How are you with a musket? There are things to shoot at. Thousands of brown ones."

"Passable, sir."

"You will learn quickly. Your life will depend upon it."

Pizarro stepped back, but kept regarding me. He was old enough to be my grandfather, a man sixty or more, wearing a scanty black beard threaded with gray, erect, narrow at the shoulders, stiff in his movements, and very small.

It was his eyes that held you. Black, penetrating, the eyes of a man quick to fury, and yet there was about them a trace of sadness, as if what he had seen had left him unsatisfied, a look of resentment that I didn't understand until much later, when I heard from his own lips that he had been born in a pigsty to an unwed mother, a bastard child whom life had buffeted about.

"Why do you wish to join this expedition? No *jira,* no picnic this one. I have made two journeys into Peruvian lands and have left more men there in the Indian wilds than I ever brought back. What is the purpose? What will hold you together when the trail grows steep?"

"Gold," I said promptly. "There's enough in Peru, I hear, to meet the needs of all the kings in creation."

"Not adventure?"

"I've seen enough adventure."

"Good! Adventure wears thin. It rusts. Gold does not."

I was certain that I detected in his words a hint that gold, no matter how much, would never satisfy him. And that deep in the glance he cast upon me was some soaring ambition that even his recently gained title of Governor-General of New Castile did not satisfy. Time proved me right!

•
• •

The next morning at dawn Pizarro gathered his forces, which numbered less than two hundred men, and celebrated the feast day of St. John the Evangelist. Under a clear sky and a favorable wind we then embarked for Peru, land of the Inca. I held the tiller of the largest of the three caravels.

We sailed for thirteen days, held back by contrary currents. In the Bay of St. Matthew, Pizarro went ashore with his men while our ships continued on course some distance from the coast.

After two weeks of sailing we sighted Pizarro again, loaded down now with gold and silver he had taken from the Indians during his march south. The treasure was divided among his men; *la quinta* taken out for King Carlos the Fifth was put aboard; and the fleet, to my great disappointment, was sent back to Panamá to deliver the king's share to the royal treasurer.

We sailed south once more, taking with us, in addition to twenty recruits, the royal inspector and a host of high officers appointed by the crown to oversee Pizarro's adventure. I began to wonder if my lot was to be a permanent steersman between Panamá and Peru, hauling traffic back and forth, transporting casks of gold and silver in which so far I had no share.

On the twenty-fourth of September, in the year 1532, I left the ship, walked up the beach into the small settlement of

San Miguel, which had been established to house the king's officials, and presented myself to Pizarro.

He was standing in the plaza listening to the royal *veedor,* inspector of all gold and silver, who was waving his hands, explaining something or other. Pizarro's beard was neatly trimmed and he wore a clean red doublet. There was no sign that he had just finished a long hard journey through hostile country.

I would like to report that Pizarro smiled, pleased to find me there. The opposite is true.

"You haven't been paid," he said. "You are here to complain, like the others. Jesú Maria, will it never end!"

"I am not here to complain about the gold," I said, "although I have hauled tons of it to Panamá and not seen so much as a pebble that I could call my own. I have left my job as steersman and wish to enlist in your army."

"You have a soft job and you give it up?" he said. "You won't last long against the Indians. You're far too big a target for their arrows, but you have that look in your eye. Come and be cured of it. You'll get armor over there by the church, and as soon as one of the cavalry dies I'll have a horse for you."

I received the horse sooner than expected. That night a cavalryman — the same Tomás Calderón who had chased the Indians out of La Perla — was killed in a brawl over dice. His horse was in good health and of fair dimensions, though not to be compared in any way to my stallion, Bravo.

We left at noon, I riding at the fore, carrying a flag emblazoned with the black eagle of the royal arms. It was an uncomfortable place to be, but Pizarro put me there, saying that my demeanor would impress the Indians, give them second thoughts.

Under a cloudless sky we headed south into the foothills of the mighty Andes. Every man of our little army — the one hundred ten on foot and the sixty-seven on horseback — was in high spirits. We knew where we were bound. Somewhere in the vast country that stretched before us, in the mountains piled upon mountains of Peru, lived Inca Atahualpa, ruler of all things beheld and not beheld by him, and, friend or foe, of our destinies.

His signs, as we went forward, were everywhere. We passed canals that brought water from the mountain streams and spread it in a network over orchards and grain fields. We traveled comfortably on a raised causeway and at every place of any size a royal caravansary was available to house us at night, as it housed the Inca when he was traveling through his domain. We also saw in several hamlets evidence of his iron hand — dead men hanging by their heels.

On the fourth and fifth days after leaving San Miguel, the country changed. We went through a series of wild ravines so steep that the horsemen had to dismount and walk, then crossed a river where we lost two horses. On the fifth day, noting that some of his men had lost their enthusiasm for the journey and had begun to complain among themselves, Pizarro called a halt.

"A crisis," he said, "has arisen that demands all our courage. No man should think of going forward in the expedition who cannot do so with his whole heart. If any of you have misgivings it is not too late to turn back. San Miguel is poorly garrisoned and I would be glad to see it in greater strength."

It was a bold challenge and a desperate one, for he had no way of knowing how many of his army would choose to leave. Six, a dozen, more? It reminded me of Cortés' rash act on the beach at Vera Cruz, when in front of his men he set fire to his ships, thus cutting off all chance of retreat, and set their faces toward Tenochtitlán and Moctezuma.

There were nine in all who chose to return to San Miguel. We set off without them, reaching on the next day a place called Zaran, situated in a fruitful valley among the mountains. Its narrow streets were almost deserted, due, according to the Indians who remained, to a levy Atahualpa had made upon them.

We took a southerly course, which led through a succession of hamlets, also deserted, and came to a wide river. Fearing an ambush on the far side, Pizarro sent his half-brother Hernán under cover of night to secure a safe landing. The next morning we hewed timber and built a floating bridge, and by nightfall the whole company passed over it, the horses swimming, led by the bridle.

Before us, outlined against the fading sky, rose the Andes, so far into the heavens that the snow covering their crests must have lain upon them for centuries, never melting from one year to the next.

"They shut out half the sky," Pizarro gasped and we all gasped with him.

His half-brother said, "It will take us years to climb the *bastardes*."

"We'll be old before we ever see Cajamarca," Hernán de Soto said.

"Not old," said Felipillo, Pizarro's Indian interpreter, who complained even when the trail was level. "Dead. Dead, and our white bones scattered everywhere."

"Yours," Pizarro said, "will not be white."

"Why do you say that?" Felipillo asked.

"Because you're a little savage," Pizarro said. "Savage bones are always brown, not white."

Father Valverde, a Dominican who had attached himself to us at San Miguel, pointed to a broad causeway. "That friendly road lined with trees takes us to Cuzco," he said.

"Cuzco in Inca words means 'navel,' " Felipillo added. "The navel is where the gold hides."

"Indians have told me the same," I said, loud enough for Pizarro to hear.

"How do you know what the Indians say?" he asked me. "You don't speak Inca."

"I've learned much on the journey."

"From me," Felipillo said, pointing to himself. "I am the best teacher of those who know nothing."

Pizarro said, "We have proclaimed to everyone that we intend to visit the Inca's camp in Cajamarca. If we turn away now, he would accuse us of cowardice and treat us with contempt. Take heart. Doubt not that God will humble the pride of the heathen and bring him to the knowledge of the true faith, the great end and object of our conquest."

I was surprised that he had decided upon a different appeal from any he had used before. He spoke not a word about the great adventure we were embarked upon. He gave no hint that we were conquistadores sent out to conquer half the world. There was no mention of the fabulous treasures that lay beyond the mountains. Suddenly we were God's soldiers fighting a war against the savage.

It rang false to me — this sudden interest in God and faith — but not at all to my comrades. "Lead on," they answered from their hearts, "lead wherever you think best."

Near dawn we set off to climb the soaring Cordillera. I rode in the lead, carrying the black eagle flag to impress any Indians we might encounter. The way was tortuous — rocky hills piled upon rocky hills, ravines aslant deep ravines; the trail, strewn with flintlike stone that cut the horses' hooves, so narrow that three of our mounts tumbled to their deaths.

On the second day the wind grew sharp. Father Valverde, who was not a young man, fell ill from the thin air. Wishing to appear humble, he had walked each step of the way since we left the sea. I gave him my horse and, fearful that he would fall off the trail, walked beside him and held the reins.

"That is a beautiful ring you wear," he said before we had gone far. "It reminds me of a ring my dear friend Bishop Pedroza wore when I saw him last. In Spain, it was, just before he embarked upon his last journey. A great man, Pedroza."

Father Valverde intended to say more, but he ran out of breath, wheezed a few words that I couldn't catch, and became silent. He did not mention the ring again until weeks later.

We reached the summit after two days and started down the far side of the Cordillera. We had not gone far when a noble appeared with a number of lordly attendants, bearing a gift of jars of a heady perfume made from dried goose fat. While he was bragging about Atahualpa and quaffing *chiche* from a golden goblet, an Indian messenger Pizarro had sent to the Inca returned to say that he had been poorly received, told that he could not see the Inca, and barely allowed to escape with his life. The city was all but deserted, he said.

At this news, Pizarro stormed at the envoy, upbraiding him for the Inca's bad manners. For which the envoy coldly apologized, informing the general that this was the season when the Inca was occupied with solemn religious duties and could see no one. The city was deserted because the Inca wished to make room for the white men who were about to occupy it.

Pizarro took these words gracefully and apologized in turn, but underneath he was greatly disturbed, as we all were. We had distrusted Atahualpa. This latest incident added fuel to our suspicions.

The descent of the wild Cordillera began at once.

•
•••

After seven days of hard travel on trails nearly as tortuous as those we had encountered on our ascent of the Cordillera, our little band came in view of Cajamarca. The morning was cloudless. The approaches to the city stood out sharply under a bright Inca sun.

We looked down upon a valley round in shape, five leagues in length and nearly five in breadth. The river we had followed out of the mountains flowed down through this large expanse in a series of loops, and from it a network of canals branched off into green fields and orchards.

Beyond the valley, in a declivity surrounded by low hills, lay Cajamarca. Its flat-roofed houses, washed with coatings of lime, all more or less the same, like cells in a honeycomb, were not impressive. It was what lay beyond the city that made us gape.

For most of two leagues, well past the range of our eyes, stretched symmetrical rows of tents and pavilions in different, barbaric colors with flags flying above them, and above them birdlike kites twisting high in the air. It was the encampment of Inca Atahualpa and his legions.

Our band halted. For a while no one spoke. Then Pizarro said in a quiet voice, "Close your eyes to what you behold. It is far too late to turn back."

He said no more. Dividing the band into three divisions, he

sent us forward at a military pace down the slopes to the gates of the city.

No one came to greet us except one small, pink-eyed dog, who attached himself to my horse. As we passed through the gates I saw that the streets were deserted. I heard no sounds save a few scattered bird calls, now an owl, then a blue jay, sounds that I could tell came not from birds but from human throats.

The day had started off cloudless. Now a gray sky pressed down upon the deserted city, giving it a desolate look, even though fountains were spouting everywhere around the sides of an immense plaza and in its center. Triangular in shape, the plaza was fronted by low buildings with large wooden doors. These, we learned, were used as barracks for the Inca's men.

On its far side was a stairway leading to a stone fortress. Beyond, commanding the city, stood a second fortress with a high stone wall that spiraled around it. Over the top of the wall, I caught a glimpse of Atahualpa's tents in the distance, ranged among the hills.

The sky opened and freezing rain began to fall, then the rain changed to hail that bounced on the cobblestones. Despite the storm, Pizarro decided to send emissaries to meet with Atahualpa. He chose for this Hernán de Soto, his most dependable captain, and fifteen horsemen, who started off at once. He then decided that this band was too small, should the Inca prove unfriendly, and ordered twenty more of us to follow.

A league beyond the city we came to the first of the Inca's strongholds — a line of warriors standing in front of their colored tents, long spears fixed in the ground. There were no signs from them as we trotted past with friendly waves and a blast of trumpets.

We came to a wide stream that appeared to be the second of the Inca's defenses. It was spanned by a wooden bridge, but distrusting its safety, de Soto took us through the stream at a gallop. On the far bank we were met by a squad of heavily armed Indians, too astonished by our appearance to reply to questions. At last, emboldened by our captain's smiles, one of their number pointed out the imperial camp.

It was a rambling pleasure retreat, not a camp or fortress, of many galleries leading into a spacious courtyard with a large pool from which hot vapor rose in clouds. At one end of the courtyard, as we rode through the gateway, was a cluster of nobles. In their midst, under a canopy that protected him from the storm, sat Atahualpa.

In Spain I had seen a picture of a Moorish potentate seated among cushions, surrounded by his courtly attendants. It was this picture that leaped to mind as I stood looking down upon the Inca.

Pizarro had chosen me over Felipillo, since I was a towering Spaniard, to translate his greetings. Which I did by getting down from my horse and saying that we had come in peace, sent hither by a mighty king to offer him blessings and to impart the doctrines of the true faith.

"Also," I said in closing my little speech, "the king's emissary, Francisco Pizarro, wishes to invite you to the quarters he presently occupies in the city of Cajamarca."

The words had barely left my mouth when Felipillo burst forth to correct a mistake I had made with my tenses.

The Inca answered neither of us. He sat among his cushions looking off at the sky, which was now beginning to clear. He was a young man and very handsome. In contrast to his nobles, who looked like tropical birds in their finery, he was dressed in a simple white garment. The only mark of his kingship was a crimson fringe, which he wore on his forehead.

At last one of the nobles standing at his side said, "It is well."

I translated the words for our captain, de Soto, who received them with some confusion, not knowing what they meant, whether they were friendly or not. He then asked me to tell the Inca to speak not through the mouth of someone else, but through his own mouth.

The Inca roused himself. "Tell your captain," he said to me, speaking with the faintest of smiles, "that I am keeping a fast, which will end tomorrow. I will then visit him with my chieftains. In the meantime, let him occupy the public buildings on the square, and no other, till I come, when I will order what shall be done."

De Soto was angry at this reply. There was an awkward silence as the two men stared at each other. To ease the situation and in doing so to impress Atahualpa, de Soto put spurs to his horse, circled the courtyard at a reckless pace, sped through the gateway, came back, and wheeled his mount around, finally bringing him to a rearing halt in front of the monarch, so close that flecks of foam spattered the royal garments.

While this took place, my eye was caught by a girl of fifteen or sixteen who stood to one side of the seated monarch, holding a woman's hand. There were a dozen or more women clustered to one side of him — all of them Atahualpa's wives, I was to learn — but the woman nearest him was his favorite, and the girl his most beloved daughter.

She seemed more like the Inca than her mother. She had his eyes, dark and deeply set above wide cheekbones, yet her glance was not imperious like his.

When de Soto was finished with his antics and had rejoined our ranks, Atahualpa ordered refreshments to be served to all our men, including warm *chiche* in gold goblets so huge that they were difficult to hold and drink from.

Indeed, I was more interested in the goblet than I was in the *chiche*. Shaped like an alligator, the long tail serving as a handle and the open jaws as the bowl, it was a bizarre yet beautiful object. But more remarkable than its beauty was its size. It must have weighed all of twenty pounds.

Each time I lifted it to my mouth, I paused, overcome by its weight. There were nearly forty men in our little army, and every one of them had a heavy alligator goblet. What munificence! What stocks of gold the Inca must have hidden away in his secret storehouses!

The girl with her father's dark eyes, but not his imperious look, whose black hair was combed into ringlets and tied with golden bells, kept watching me as I toyed with the *chiche*. She seemed amused.

Embarrassed, I finally drank down the *chiche* in one long gulp, wiped my mouth, and returned her look. During this time Atahualpa, who had been chewing on a mouthful of pink nuts, decided that it was time to spit. He motioned to his favorite wife, who came forward and held out her open hand for him to spit into.

While this intimate act took place, emboldened by the fiery *chiche,* I approached the girl, made a deep genuflection copied from the Inca bows I had observed — I even touched my forehead to the stones — and asked her name.

She spoke without any sign of shyness. "Chima," she said, and followed it by several names I didn't catch, ending with "Atahualpa," which she spoke proudly.

"Chima Atahualpa," I said, skipping all the titles in between and increasingly emboldened, "you have a very pretty name and everything that goes with a pretty name."

Bold words to address to an Inca princess. I glanced at her father to see if he had heard. He was busy spitting.

The girl smiled, whether to show her even rows of small white teeth — startlingly white against her dusky skin — or to thank me for the compliment, I did not know. She glanced at the goblet, which I clasped in both hands.

"You are full of excitement about the goblet, aren't you?"

she said. "It is pretty, isn't it? It is made by our finest craftsmen. Far away from here. In Cuzco. My father always gives one to each of his guests when they leave. He will give one to you."

I nodded my thanks and would have spoken then had I not been on my knees, not an arm's length from the Indian girl. A wild, unknown scent came from her that assailed my nostrils. But it was not the scent. Looking back at this moment, I believe something in her gaze suddenly reminded me of Selka Mulamé. A feeling of sadness at my last days in Quintana swept over me.

The memory and the sadness quickly faded, and I was visited by a feeling I had experienced only once before in my lifetime.

It was on the morning when I knelt in the church of San Gil, before La Macarena, Virgin of Hope. She was the protectress of bullfighters — a matador would never think of going near a ring without her blessing. I was aged twelve and had no thought of ever fighting a bull, but I had friends who did think about it. I went with them to kneel before her on a Sunday morning, pretending that I was a matador and had come here before all of my dangerous *corridas*.

La Macarena wore priceless jewels in her hair and around her neck and on her bodice. They dazzled my eyes, but it was her face that moved me. She had pink cheeks and a mouth like a rosebud that has just begun to open. But it was not these things. It was her eyes. I was so entranced by them that my friends left me kneeling there in the church and went on their way.

The little princess had a different face from that of the Virgin of Hope, not rounded and pink, and her mouth was not a rosebud. It was her eyes that were the same as the Virgin's. Large, black, flecked with amber — a midnight color — they enthralled me.

I forgot where I was, and for an instant I was again in Seville kneeling before La Macarena. I heard a shout from de Soto and turned in time to see the last of the troops leave the courtyard. Hurriedly getting to my feet, wordlessly bowing to the girl, I jumped on my horse and fled. Overtaking my friends, I was greeted by jibes, to which I made no reply.

When we reached Cajamarca and looked back, we saw that thousands of watch fires had begun to show on the hill-sides. "They're as thick as the stars of heaven," Pizarro observed.

At once he called a council of his officers, Father Valverde, Felipillo, and myself.

"We're faced with appalling danger," he said to us. "We're surrounded by danger. But it is too late now to fly. And whither could we fly? At the first sign of retreat, the whole Inca army would be upon us. The causeways, the roads, the passes through the mountains would be occupied. We would be hemmed in on all sides."

Yet for all these serious words, Pizarro seemed lighthearted. He limped back and forth through the room, his eyes flashing in the light of a fire we fed with the Inca's furniture.

"We have been decoyed across the mountains," he said, "a step at a time. We are now in the net Atahualpa has artfully prepared for us. Yet we have time, a day perhaps, to escape it. Not by fleeing his fury, but by turning fury upon him."

He went on to describe his plans at length, even to such small details as the fixing of bells to the horses' breastplates in order to startle the Indians when the fighting began. The plan was similar to the barbarous attack Cortés had carried out at Cholólan and of his captain, Alvarado, at Tenochtitlán.

It was well past midnight when the council broke up. Sentinels were posted at the gateway to the city and on the roof of the main fortress. We then bedded down in the quarters Atahualpa had prepared for us.

Sleep came slowly. I kept hearing bird calls, the same calls I had heard when we entered the city, hours before. However, it was not danger that kept me awake. It was the dark gaze of Chima Atahualpa and her wild, flowery scent. And the sound of the little bells when she moved her head.

•
• • • •

The storm ended during the night. In the morning Father Valverde celebrated a solemn mass, and everyone joined in the fervent chant, "Rise, O Lord, and judge thine own cause." The chant went on and on and grew in volume until it was shortened by exhausted throats to *"Exsurge Domine."* I was kneeling to the fore, not far from Valverde, when, looking up from his book, he made a note that I was taking no part in the chant.

After the service was over he sought me out. "You don't wish the Lord to join our cause?" he said.

There were no differences between me and Father Valverde — none that I was aware of — and I wanted none. Since the day on the trail when he spoke about the amethyst ring and said that Pedroza was a dear friend, I had viewed him with suspicion. He reminded me of that hard-headed, martyrdom-seeking bishop.

"On the contrary," I said. "I devoutly wish that the Lord will help us." I could not say and still remain in camp, "Help us all, the Indians especially."

"Then why did you not join our humble plea to the Lord in this hour of peril?"

"Because," I lied with a serious face, "my voice is not suited at all for chanting. Or for singing, either. Even my speaking voice, as you may have heard, has an unpleasing twinge to it.

The results of a boyhood brawl, in which I was at fault, sir."

"The Lord," Valverde replied, "listens to all sounds. Be they croaks, squeals, or grunts. He hears all."

"Then next time, sir, I'll be bold and add my humble voice to the chants."

"There will be no next time," Valverde said with godly confidence, froth clinging to his lips. "The heathen savage and his minions shall be vanquished, scattered to the four winds of the world."

Father Vincente de Valverde, chaplain and spiritual adviser to Francisco Pizarro, was right — there was no "next time" for Atahualpa and his people, ever again.

Late that afternoon, before sunset, the Inca led a royal procession through the gates of the city. Hundreds of menials with hundreds of brooms swept every hindrance from his path, singing songs of triumph as they came.

"They sound," Father Valverde remarked, "like songs hatched in hell."

The procession filled the square, which was twice as large as the largest square in Seville. Atahualpa rode high above everyone, in an open litter lined with the plumes of tropical birds and shining plates of gold and silver. In the very center of the square, he halted and glanced around at his vassals, who by now numbered seven thousand or more.

"Where are the strangers?" he shouted in a voice that carried to us as we stood hidden behind the stone walls of the barracks. "Strangers, come forth, I have not a whole day to talk."

At this moment Father Valverde strode forward with Little Philip, and I followed at their heels. The crowds divided before us. No voice was raised. There was not a sound as we made our way to where the Inca stood waiting beside his litter.

Valverde carried a Bible in one hand and a crucifix in the other. He held the crucifix at arm's length toward Atahualpa, as if to ward off evil spirits, and then spoke quickly in a dry voice, as Felipillo and I took turns changing his Spanish to the language of Peru.

It was a long recital, beginning with the fall of man and his redemption by Jesus Christ. After every sentence I picked up the priest's words and as best I could translated them for Atahualpa.

He stood only a few paces away from us, a regal figure in his long white gown and collar of flashing emeralds. He seemed to understand little of what I said, but when Felipillo took over the task of translating he began to listen more intently.

At times he smiled and nodded his head. But at the end, hearing Valverde's final demand, spoken in a rising voice and clearly explained by Little Philip, that he must acknowledge the supremacy of the Christian faith and the power of the Spanish king, he raised his hand in a menacing gesture and suddenly took a step toward us.

"I will be no man's tributary," he shouted. "I am willing to hold your emperor as a brother, but not as one who gives me commands. For my faith, I will not change it."

He paused to glance back at the nobles who stood behind him, adding their outrage to his own. When they were silent he spoke in a quiet voice.

"Your own God was put to death by the very men He created," the Inca said and pointed to the sun. "But mine still lives in the heavens and looks down on his children." Then he turned to Valverde. "By what authority do you say these things and make these demands?"

Valverde thrust the Bible toward him. The Inca took it and ruffled the pages, muttering to himself as his face darkened.

"Go tell your comrades," he said, "that they shall give me a full account of their doings in my land. And that I shall not go forth from here until they do."

With these angry words, he flung the Bible at Valverde's

feet. The priest picked up the holy book, pawed his way through the crowd, and I followed him. Pizarro was waiting inside the barracks door.

"Did you not see," Valverde cried out, "that while I stood there talking to this dog, full of pride as he is, the square and the fields beyond filled with savages?"

"I have seen it all," Pizarro said.

"Then act, I pray you," Valverde said.

Pizarro said nothing. It was at this moment that I should have spoken. Not that any word from me, or a thousand words, could have stayed his hand. The plan had been thought out, was complete. Nothing, no one, could have changed it — not Valverde, not King Carlos himself.

Yet if I had raised my voice against the dark act it would have given me peace of mind, at least, for to be silent in the face of evil is to condone it. It was out of cowardice that I held my tongue. To have set myself against Pizarro would have meant my death.

"The time is now," Valverde said.

"It is past the time," Pizarro said. "It is late."

"Not too late," Valverde said. "Set on at once. I absolve you."

Pizarro was not waiting for absolution, only for himself. At last he waved a white scarf — the agreed-upon sign. A falconet was fired from the roof of the fortress, and men poured into the square, shouting, "Santiago, and at them!"

The massacre lasted for nearly an hour. The Indians who tried to escape were hacked down. Their bodies piled up and choked the gateway. Some broke through the wall that enclosed the square and fled into the countryside. Others were cut down by the horsemen or trampled to death.

My own part in the hideous act was small and very confused. At the first rush I rode out with Pizarro to be on hand if he saw fit to talk to Atahualpa. I had no thought of using the sword, yet I couldn't keep from trampling the Indians in the stallion's path.

I found myself near the center of the square, not far from Pizarro, who was trying to reach Atahualpa, and surrounded by a flood of fleeing bodies, when a young Indian became entangled in my reins. We looked at each other in surprise — two strangers who had accidentally bumped together in the street.

For an instant I thought he was about to apologize. Then I saw that it wasn't an accident. The man had a good hold on the reins and was putting all his weight on them. Suddenly, as the stallion reared, he was lifted from the ground. He swung in the air but held on. The reins were wrapped around one of his wrists.

"Let go, you fool," I shouted above the din, fighting to keep my seat in the saddle.

The Indian said nothing. He wore heavy gold rings in his ears — a sign of nobility — and his bare chest was painted with bars and circles. His hand had turned white from the pressure of the reins wrapped around his wrist.

"Let go," I shouted again.

In answer he took a grip on the reins with his other hand. He was on his feet one moment and in the air, his feet dangling, the next. He carried no weapons in his breechclout. He was bent upon only one thing — unseating me, dragging me to the ground.

Above the din of screams and moans and the neighing of horses, leaning toward him so that our bodies almost touched, I shouted in his face, "Let go, Inca, or I will kill you."

His hold on the reins loosened, and I thought that he wanted to let me go. But then he took another grip and as he did so, swung toward me and spat upon my chest.

The sword was rusted to its sheath. I yanked it free and lunged at him. The heavy blade fell across his wrists. He stared up at me for a fleeting moment, as if he was surprised that I really meant the blow. A second blow severed his hands, and he staggered away and was lost in the crowd.

I found Pizarro. He was still working his way toward Atahualpa. The air was gray with smoke from our muskets and falconets.

We reached the center of the square. Atahualpa was in his litter, enclosed by a band of nobles who had no weapons but were protecting him with their bodies. As we came upon him, the litter was overborne and he was thrown to the ground. Swordsmen rushed to finish him off. Pizarro stopped them.

"Let no man strike the Inca," he shouted. "On pain of death!"

Like the massacres at Cholólan, when Cortés destroyed the city, and at Tenochtitlán, when Alvarado slew most of the Aztéca nobles, this slaughter ended at sundown. By rough count, Pizarro and his soldiers on that day killed more than six thousand in the town of Cajamarca and wounded half that number.

Pizarro saved Inca Atahualpa from the swords, not out of sympathy, but because he was far more important to him alive than dead. Before dusk settled on the square, while the last of the Indians were being hunted down, he whisked Atahualpa from the mob and led him to safety.

That night Pizarro held a banquet for the emperor in one of the halls facing the great plaza, the scene only hours before of the massacre. Moans of the dying could be heard as we sat down to eat. With Little Philip seated next to me, eager to correct any mistakes I might make, I translated Pizarro's words to the stunned emperor.

"I beseech you," Pizarro said to him in the gentlest and most pleading of voices, "not to be downcast by what has befallen you. Similar misfortunes have befallen all those who have resisted us."

Atahualpa, who sat across the table from me, received these words, which were meant to be comforting, in stunned silence. He was a broad-shouldered, rugged man of thirty or less, much larger than the nobles around him, with a hawklike eye and the proud bearing of an emperor.

"We have come to this land," Pizarro went on, "to proclaim the creed of Jesus Christ. It is small wonder, therefore, that He has protected us. And that heaven itself has allowed your pride to be humbled because of your hostile thoughts about us. As well as the insult you offered to our sacred book, the Bible."

Atahualpa's expression didn't change at these words. He was sitting next to Pizarro and never glanced at him. His eyes were on me, watching every word that came from my mouth, as if they came not from his conqueror but from me.

"And yet, my friend, I ask you to take courage," Pizarro said. "We Spaniards are a generous race, warring only against those who war against us. We wish to show grace toward all who submit."

As I finished with these words, silence fell upon the hall, and I heard the cries of the wounded who were lying in the square. Pizarro heard them also, crossed himself, and waited for the Inca to answer. The Inca said nothing. And when the others at the table drank and began to eat, he sat gravely, his jeweled hands clasped in his lap.

Father Valverde, seeing that I was troubled by the sounds that came from the square, whispered in my ear.

"Remember," he said, "that Charlemagne converted the Germans by hanging ten thousand of them." He paused to drink from the golden goblet he had been given the previous day. "We shall do this in Peru also, God willing."

•

That night, after the banquet, Pizarro warned us that we were still in the heart of a powerful kingdom, surrounded by foes who were deeply attached to their emperor. We must be ever on guard, he said, ready to spring from our slumbers at the first call of the trumpet. He then posted sentinels throughout the town and placed a heavy guard on the chambers of Atahualpa.

In the morning the prisoners were set to work digging trenches outside the walls, in which they were told to bury their dead. A troop of thirty horsemen was sent to the Inca's pleasure-house to gather up all the spoils it could find, to kill or drive off any nobles who still clung to the place. Captain Alvarado led the troop and I went with him to serve as interpreter.

We arrived in midmorning to find the gate open but the courtyard deserted. Not until a trumpet had been sounded and a musket fired did a fat, elderly nobleman appear, bowing deeply each step or two as he came toward us.

"There is no one here except me, Pacha Camac," he said in a feeble voice. "Me and the wives and children of Inca Atahualpa. What is it that you desire?"

"We desire," Alvarado said, "gold and silver and emeralds. Jewelry of value. Rich fabrics. And we desire these things without delay. Stir yourself, or else it will go hard with you."

He added a few insults to his speech, none of which I translated. The troopers did not wait for the old man to answer. They were already in the pleasure-house, running from room to room.

Shortly thereafter, as the first of the troopers appeared with armloads of treasure and piled them in the courtyard under the watchful eye of Alvarado, I heard the rustle of a dress and glanced around to find someone standing behind me.

The sun was in my eyes and until she spoke I didn't see that it was Chima, Atahualpa's daughter. Her face had changed. Her hair was done neatly, but not with the tinkling bells she had worn when we had met before. In her hands, clutched to her breasts, was a golden cup.

"You didn't remember when you went away to take this with you," she said.

"Yes, in all the excitement I forgot."

"I saved it for you," she said. "Just now someone tried to take it from me — one of your men — but I screamed and drove him off. Did you hear me then?"

I was too embarrassed to answer. My tongue clove to my mouth. I wanted to fall to my knees and beg forgiveness for the disaster Pizarro had visited upon her father, upon her people, upon the girl herself.

"This is a dark time," she said.

"Dark." I managed to repeat the word. "Dark."

"Do you think the dark will go away?" she said.

Chima spoke without the least hint of anger. I marveled that she could. Thousands of her people slain, her father held captive, her home at this very moment being ransacked by a band of gold-mad adventurers, their shouts echoing in the courtyard. The treasure they hauled out piece by piece, like frantic ants, was growing rapidly before her eyes.

"Will these men go away?" she said.

"Yes," I said, still appalled, still at a loss for words. "When they have all the gold they can carry, they will go. They and the darkness together," I said, not to comfort her, for she apparently was in no need of comfort. "Soon."

I was amazed that she still showed no emotion. She looked older, a year older, than when I had seen her last, but there was nothing in her voice to betray the sorrow she must feel. And yet, it was possible that she felt nothing. After all, her father had sat through the banquet without a trace of emotion. I remembered that Moctezuma had watched his kingdom slip away with scarcely a word, accepting his fate because it was ordained. Chima could feel the same — that her fate was likewise ordained.

She held out the golden cup. I hesitated to take it.

"You admired it the other day here in the courtyard," she said with a touch of spirit, the first I had heard from her. "You almost forgot to drink because you admired it so much."

"The beauty is what I admired." She knew I was lying and showed it by the hint of a smile.

"You did forget the cup," she said. "You put it down and went away, although you did admire it. I saw your eyes shine."

"I admired you more," I said. "That's why I forgot and left the cup behind."

Having said this, I was silent, astounded at myself. The words seemed to hover above her, sharp and clear, a wreath of flowers of all colors. Her face seemed to be the face of La Macarena. Then my blood went rushing through me so loud I could hear it. I was dumb with fright, gazing with words again stuck to my tongue at the most beautiful girl I had ever seen. Miracles have never been explained. All we know is that they happen when least expected as a sign of Christ's love.

The stored treasure now was piled high in the courtyard, and a noisy argument had broken out among the troopers. Some, who thought that the Inca had hidden most of his gold, were for tying the old nobleman to the tail of a horse and dragging the truth out of him, as I had seen it done at Chichén-Palapa.

The girl heard the shouts. "I know my father is a prisoner in Cajamarca. The news came this morning. Will he be harmed by these men, do you think?"

There was fear in her voice, the first I had heard. "Pizarro is in command at Cajamarca," I said. "He can be trusted to protect your father."

I said this with all the conviction I could muster, knowing full well that Pizarro would do only what was in his interests. He was a man without scruples, fear of God or the devil. He certainly would put Atahualpa to the torture should the need arise.

The argument between the troopers grew more heated. One of them seized the old man by the throat and would have choked him had I not intervened. For my efforts, I received a painful bruise; when I went back to the garden where Chima and I had been talking, I found her gone.

Soon afterward she appeared riding with her mother. They were in a red litter supported on the shoulders of a dozen men. In their wake came other litters, carrying other women, a crowd of menials on foot, a herd of llamas burdened with clothes and household goods, and a long line of unarmed guards. It took most of an hour for the caravan to take the trail to Cajamarca.

Meanwhile the pleasure-house was now empty. The troopers left nothing behind. The gold and silver were loaded on the horses, the other less valuable things were bundled up and carried by a flock of llamas that Alvarado had collected nearby.

We passed the Incas before we reached Cajamarca. I rode up as close to the litter bearing Chima and her mother as courtesy permitted, close enough to see her receive my greeting with the faintest of smiles and follow me with her dark, troubled gaze as I rode on.

When we reached Cajamarca, I sought out Pizarro. He was at supper with his officers, not seated but limping up and down in front of them, his jaw set, stabbing the air with his forefinger, his food untouched.

"Give thought," he was saying as I sat down at the table, "to the fact that Cuzco is high in the most monstrous mountains in the world, a good three hundred leagues from where I now stand."

"But it is the center of the Inca empire," Morales, the inspector of metals, said. "It is the home of the Inca gold. It is the place where the Inca palaces outshine the sun. We waste our time in deserted Cajamarca."

Pizarro turned to Alvarado, who had followed me in. "What did you bring us?" he asked the captain.

"It is stacked in the square, sir."

"In value, how much?"

"As a guess, a thousand gold pesos."

"You got it all?"

"All, sir."

"Well, less than I expected," Pizarro said, disappointed.

I spoke up. "The Inca's wives and children and servants are on their way here. They'll arrive soon. Where will you house them?"

"Alvarado," Pizarro said, "give this your attention. We want the women and their servants treated with the utmost hospitality. How about the House of the Serpents?"

"That's where we stable the horses."

"Have it swept out," Pizarro said. "And amply furnished. We'll move Atahualpa in among his women and children. We want everyone to be respectfully treated. Happy."

I met his eyes as he spoke these last words. I saw a fierce light that told me he had already decided on a plan to wring the last ounce of gold from Inca Atahualpa.

He motioned for the servants to fill the golden cups. Limping to the table, he picked up his own and lifted it high. "To the Inca," he shouted. "To the richest king in the world." He paused, then added under his breath to himself, "Now but not forever."

He drank the toast at one long gulp. As his officers drank theirs, I raised the heavy goblet to my lips. The taste of the *chiche* was bitter. Its color — a dark brown streaked with red — looked like the blood that ran underfoot on the day of the massacre. I turned away and quietly spat it on the floor.

Among the officers at supper was a Captain Almagro. He had arrived that morning with credentials from the king that gave him the right to explore lands to the south of Peru. But he didn't speak of exploration during the meal. He was interested in the gold Pizarro had collected, and because he had stationed himself in San Miguel for months protecting Pizarro's interests and was now present with a band of well-armed soldiers, he demanded a share of the treasure.

Pizarro treated him politely, said that there was more than enough gold for everyone, but when the meal was over he led me outside and asked what had taken place at the Inca's pleasure-house.

"Alvarado claims to have collected only a thousand gold pesos in goods today," he said. "What value would you give them?"

"I am not a goldsmith," I said.

"As a guess."

"A thousand gold pesos."

"Did Alvarado collect all?"

"Everything."

"He left nothing behind?"

"A few dogs."

"Nothing was hidden along the trail on your way back?"

"Nothing that I saw."

His men had quarreled for months now over the division

of treasure, envying King Carlos his royal share, suspicious of each other, suspicious of Pizarro himself. But this was the first time I had heard Pizarro doubt the honesty of one of his own officers.

"The buzzards gather," he said. "Soon they will darken the heavens. Someday soon there will be more buzzards than gold."

While we talked in the dusk the caravan of women entered the square, led by a *mayordomo* resplendent in gold and feathers, flanked by torchbearers. In their midst were two musicians, one with a thin flute and the other with a deep-voiced drum.

The caravan stopped in the square, not far from us, and Pizarro sent me out to direct the *mayordomo* to the House of the Serpents, which I did, pointing to a vast, low-lying structure on the far side of the square, where fires had begun to show.

I stood aside as the caravan passed, the long line of menials now walking in front, sweeping a pathway as they went. Night had fallen. The litter that carried the princess and her mother slipped by me without a sound. The reed curtains were drawn and I caught not the smallest glimpse of the girl.

My heart was pounding as I walked back to where Pizarro brooded, in the light of a lantern a servant had brought him. He was moving up and down, dragging one foot, muttering to himself.

"Yesterday," he said, "it was news from the scoundrel Ibañez. Today it's Almagro, a gentleman. Gentlemen are hard to refuse — they make you think that God is watching when He really isn't. God is not concerned with gold — with nothing, as far as I can see. Now that He's set everything in motion, like a child's top of many colors, it's up to us humans to make the most of it. Life's a blur, señor, a spinning puzzle with many answers. You're lucky, *amigo,* if in a long life you find just one."

He stopped pacing. In the lantern light I saw that although the night was cold, drops of sweat stood on his brow.

"My own men quarrel among themselves," he said. "My officers, the king's inspectors, even Father Valverde, scheme to slit Pizarro's purse. They drain his blood with their sharp claws."

"Divide the gold," I said.

"And take the edge off their appetites? I wish to keep them hungry. There's more out there in Peru, ten times a hundred, yet to be gathered."

"Their appetites will be all the keener once they have a taste of the feast."

"Young man, you don't know the rules of human greed."

He began to pace again, swinging the lantern, muttering to himself about *zopilotes* that darkened the heavens with their soft black wings. He was a man possessed.

I glanced across the square. In the tower high in the House of the Serpents, where Atahualpa often lived before Pizarro arrived, I saw that a fire was burning. The girl was there now, warming herself against the cold, pale and frightened of what the next day would bring. The firelight made a path across the stones. It somehow joined us together in the dark night.

Pizarro shone the lantern in my face. "Why do you stare into the night?" he said. "What do you see there? Mounds of gold? Like the rest of the spiders, do you spin webs?"

I didn't answer. If I said, or so much as hinted, that I was appalled by his massacre of the Inca thousands, that from the hour I saw the streets of Cajamarca run deep with blood the very sight of gold had sickened me, then at this moment I would be driven from the town.

Offended by my silence, Pizarro discarded his lantern and walked away to inspect the sentries who watched from the roof and all sides of the stone prison that held the priceless hostage, Atahualpa Capac, Emperor of Peru.

Pizarro was not pleased by the booty Alvarado brought back from his raid on the pleasure-house, consisting of rich plate from the royal table and massive emeralds left behind by the slain nobles. It did not quench his thirst, nor the thirst of his officers and men, who grew more restless day by day.

The bulk of the emperor's vast treasure was yet to be found. Elsewhere, all reports agreed; in Cuzco, the cloud city high in the Andes. But Cuzco was far away. The Spanish forces were small, and many were needed to see that Atahualpa did not escape. It was dangerous to go marching off with a small force on a journey of three hundred leagues among enemy thousands, leaving a horde of prisoners behind. Some of the officers suggested that Pizarro render them helpless by cutting off their hands.

Pizarro brooded on his problems for days, then put the restless soldiers to work changing one of the Indian temples into a Christian church, thereby giving them something to think about besides gold. He also gave thought to how best to handle the caged eagle, Inca Atahualpa Capac.

Meanwhile the Inca had worries of his own. He was a prisoner, guarded night and day, well treated, encouraged to play games of dice and chess, but still a hostage facing an uncertain future. His half-brother, Huáscar, whom he had deposed as emperor, was busily collecting an army, not to use against

Pizarro but to make peace with him and thus to regain the throne he had lost.

One of these problems was suddenly solved. Mysteriously, Huáscar turned up dead — killed, some said, on Atahualpa's orders. Having taken note of Pizarro's love of gold, the Inca attempted to solve the second problem by an unusual appeal to his greed.

I first heard of this scheme when I went at Atahualpa's request as a translator for a meeting with Pizarro. I had not seen the Inca since the day of his imprisonment. His quarters, a series of gloomy rooms connected by a narrow passage, adjoined the chambers where his favorite wife and daughter were kept. Father Valverde said as we walked through the maze, "The corridors of hell must be like this. A proper place for the savage."

We found Atahualpa seated on the gold throne he had sat upon the day of the massacre, listening to a message from an Indian who had just come from Cuzco. The man was dressed in beggar's clothes, carried a small burden on his back, as tokens of respect, and spoke in the humblest of tones, though he was said to be the most powerful noble in Peru. I made out little of what he said, but judging from the few words I did understand, he was pledging undying trust in the emperor.

There were a half-dozen petitioners present, and we were kept waiting until the last had been heard — I believe deliberately to impress Pizarro. The general was both impressed and angered.

"You get the idea," he said to me, not once but twice as we waited impatiently, "that the brown man thinks he is King Carlos of Spain, Emperor of the Holy Roman Empire!"

However, when our time came, Pizarro greeted him with a low, respectful bow. In return, there was only a slight movement of the Inca's heavy lids — and I may have imagined this. He sat on his golden throne, impassive as a gold idol. He *was* an idol. He was more. He was the offspring of the sun, Lord of the Winds and Lightnings, Emperor of the Four Quarters of the World — or so he was raised to believe.

Atahualpa Inca took his time in speaking, while Pizarro stood and quietly fumed. The child of the sun, dressed all in gold cloth, wore the royal circlet on his forehead; his eyes were shielded by a green jade mask. He tilted the circlet just so, as if he were alone, making ready for a royal appearance, and carefully adjusted the mask.

"You took what you wished from my pleasure-house," he said at last. "I hear that it weighed much. I hear that it took all your beasts and a large flock of my llamas to carry it. Yet your men still ask for more. They yammer at my window. What is this sickness that besets them?"

Pizarro glanced at his polished boots, grasped his graying beard, freshly trimmed for the occasion, and said nothing.

Pizarro was a proud and arrogant man, proud that he was born of a dishonored girl, not knowing his father, a bastard raised in a pigsty, for twenty years and more driving muddy pigs down filthy streets, a ragged outcast. He could boast of all this — and often did — because he had climbed out of the mire, left it behind, become Balboa's right hand, stood with him on a peak in Darién and claimed for Spain the blue Pacific, and at this moment was known to the world as the governor-general of Peru, the fabulous land of El Dorado. Yet as he stood before the Inca, searching for an answer, he was again a bastard boy rooting in the mire, awed and uncertain.

"Do you have control over this clamor your people set up night and day like a nest of sick cats?" the Inca said.

Pizarro woke himself from self-doubt. "They have come a long distance, these men," he answered. "A greater distance ten times over than the distance from here to Cuzco. They have suffered pain and torture. They have earned a reward."

"Who asked them to come?" the Inca said. "Who asked them to suffer so much?"

"They came at the bidding of the all-powerful Emperor of Spain and of other famous lands," Pizarro said, suddenly angered, ashamed that a moment before he had acted like an ignorant pig boy. "They are here under the protection of God the Almighty to spread the word of his Son, Jesus Christ. To harvest souls in your beautiful kingdom."

"Harvest souls?" Atahualpa said contemptuously.

He studied the words, which he had heard before. I repeated them, but he shook his head.

"The Inca grows weary hearing about souls," he said. "My people have no souls to harvest. We are happy, we sun people, without souls. We are content to harvest, not souls, but our maize crops and potatoes."

"You are the great emperor of a great nation," Pizarro said, using his softest voice in a courtly manner. "However . . ."

Atahualpa interrupted him in an equally soft voice. "Great," he repeated. "My kingdom is great. An eagle can fly north and south, east and west, from the sea to the highest mountains, for days it can fly and never reach the end to Atahualpa's kingdom. I know the birds of the air. And I know my people's names, each one. I give each boy when he becomes a man a fitting parcel of land for him and his wife to hold and use and share its fruits with his neighbors, who share lands and its fruits with him likewise. They work and beget children. They are too busy to go away to other lands — there are many strange ones beyond the high mountains eastward where the vast rivers run. But we do not go there and hurt the people in the name of our god the sun. We do not go there and point a book at them with one hand and with the other a sharp sword, saying solemnly to them, 'Do this, stranger, do that, or else we'll kill you.' "

"*Absurdo,*" shouted Valverde. "We come here with love in

our hearts. We bring with us Christ's mercy and the hope of heaven. We ask little in exchange for this. Nothing, really, because you have no use for gold, except to fashion it into trinkets to adorn yourselves and your wives and your concubines."

"You tell me I place no value upon gold," Atahualpa said. "This is not true. People far from here, the Aztéca, call gold the excrement of the gods. But this is wrong. It is a bad thought. To me, Atahualpa Inca, gold is the tears of the sun, tears of happiness, which he sheds in tribute to a great kingdom."

"Enough," said Pizarro, suddenly tired of the talk. "It is also stuffed with gold, as full as a crow's crop in a blind man's cornfield. We wish our rightful share. We wish it soon."

"Now," Valverde said, "or else we shall have you burned."

It was then that Atahualpa, sensing the proper moment had come, rose from his throne chair, strode to the end of the room, and slowly returned, waving his jeweled hand, the golden bells on his sandals tinkling as he moved. He pointed to the four walls, one after the other, and to the ceiling.

"You pine for gold," he said, speaking with the arrogance of a god. "I will give it to you. I will fill this room from wall to wall and to the ceiling with gold."

Pizarro had unsheathed his sword. He put it back in the scabbard. "You'll fill this place?"

"Full," the Inca said.

Pizarro glanced around the room, which was some six paces in width and eight or nine in length. "How high?" he said.

"High," the Inca said, "higher than you, higher even than the young man who speaks for you." He made a mark on the wall that nearly reached the ceiling. "This high."

"You wish something in return," Pizarro said. "What?"

"My freedom," Atahualpa answered.

"It's a trick," Valverde said. "Beware."

"Agreed," Pizarro said at once. "You are a free man the

hour this room is filled with gold. But not a moment sooner."

Before we left him, Atahualpa had passed word of the pact to his servants. By nightfall dozens were on their way in all directions — to the treasure house of Titicata on the knife's edge of the Andes, to the gardens at Quito and Pachácamac and Xauxa, to the palaces of Arequipa and Coricaucha, to the Temple of the Virgins in the sacred city of Cuzco.

They returned slowly, too slowly for Pizarro's wishes, like a column of ants, throughout the summer, along with dozens of other servants recruited on the way, burdened under heavy loads, leading strings of llamas also burdened. They filled the room with gold from the floor to the mark Atahualpa had made on the wall. It consisted of utensils for ordinary use, dining plates, golden tiles from palace roofs, lordly earrings and ceremonial crowns, graceful statues of animals and birds, collars and necklaces, fretted figurines of the greatest delicacy.

The conquistadores cheered and drank toasts to Atahualpa Capac, Emperor of Peru. I did neither, for from the very beginning, from the moment Pizarro had said, "You are a free man the hour this room is filled with gold," I doubted that he would ever honor his promise. The perfidies of Hernán Cortés were still fresh in my mind.

My doubts were well based. Days passed and Atahualpa remained a prisoner. A week passed. Rumors spread that thousands of Indians were massed around Guamachucho, a large town to the south, sharpening their obsidian knives, praying for the Inca's return. At other towns farther away, it was said, even greater numbers had gathered.

De Soto and a band of horsemen were sent to search out the truth. Patrols were doubled. Horses were kept saddled and bridled. Soldiers slept on their arms. The general himself made the rounds at night to see that every sentinel was at his post.

Pizarro didn't wait for de Soto's return. In an angry mood he limped off to confront Atahualpa, taking me with him as usual, and to make certain that the talk was correctly translated, his other interpreter, Little Philip.

It had rained through the night and was raining hard now as we crossed the square. We all were dripping water when we broke in upon the emperor.

He was eating breakfast, seated in a nest of red cushions,

dressed in a black gown soft-looking as satin, made from the silky undersides of bat wings. Two musicians with flutes and one with a cymbal were playing a lively little tune.

At our sudden appearance the music stopped. Atahualpa glanced up and, surprised, upset a drink into his lap. A bevy of servants rushed out, set up a screen in front of him, and behind it changed him into a fresh gown, while Pizarro strode back and forth, his anger increasing.

At last the stained gown was taken away — the emperor's used clothes were always burned, never washed or worn again — and the gold screen removed. He didn't rise to greet us, but sat gazing out at the rain falling in the square, his heavy-lidded eyes serene.

The general started to speak, then changed his mind and stood awkwardly with his hands dangling, unsure of himself. He was no longer Pizarro, Governor-General of Peru, come to upbraid a culprit. His anger had vanished. Again he was the pig boy face to face with an emperor.

"I have not been freed," Atahualpa said. "Are you here to keep a promise?"

"There are reasons," Pizarro said, slurring his words, falling silent as if he had forgotten what they were.

"For a valiant man not to keep promises," Atahualpa said, "for this there can be no reasons. So I do not wish to hear them. They will sicken my stomach."

He whispered to a servant, who whispered to the musicians, and they began to play a sad little piece of tinkling notes. A servant held a gold box before him, and he took out a reddish brown nut and put it in his mouth, beside his tongue.

"Is this what comes of being a Christian man?" he said. "A breaker of promises? Is this what is taught in the book you call the Bible? Does your friend Christ teach you this?"

Pizarro flushed.

"As he has taught you to slay people for him," the emperor

added. "Nine thousand of my young men, most of them with wives and children, slain to please him. Is this what your god wishes of you? Is this the path to the heaven your Father Valverde speaks about and wishes me to take?"

He turned toward Pizarro and fixed upon him the gaze of a child who has been wronged.

Pizarro avoided his eyes and said uneasily, "You are plotting against me, me the Governor-General of Peru, your friend, who has treated you with honor. Who has believed in you as in a brother."

The emperor must have been astounded by this remark, but his expression never changed when he said to me, "Tell General Pizarro that he jests. He is always jesting with Atahualpa. How could I or my people plot against men as valiant as the Spaniards?"

The musicians had filled the room with a sudden burst of melody, which drowned out my words. Pizarro asked me to repeat them. Halfway through the translation, Little Philip burst in. He sidled up to the general.

"This devil shocks me," he said, "with his threats against you."

"Threats?" Pizarro said. "What threats?"

"He says that his soldiers plan to kill you. Soon. Tomorrow, perhaps."

Felipillo had been caught in the women's quarters a few days before, busily molesting one of the girls. Hearing of the escapade, Atahualpa had threatened to kill him. This was his way of repaying the emperor.

Little Philip had a large gap between two of his big front teeth. When planning skullduggery, he had a habit of pushing his tongue back and forth through the gap. He was doing this now, gauging how far he dare go with the general.

"Yes, the devil has bad things in his mind. Bad . . ."

I stopped Felipillo's lies by giving him a clout that sent him into a corner where he lay blinking.

Word for word I repeated what Atahualpa had said, but Pizarro was annoyed with me and did not listen. He wanted to believe Little Philip's lies, for they proved that the Inca was really plotting his destruction. He limped over and put Little Philip back on his feet.

"What else did the devil say?" Pizarro asked him.

"Much more," Little Philip whispered, "but now my head hurts and I cannot think."

Atahualpa said to Pizarro, "Am I not a captive in your hands? How could I harbor a plot when I would be the first victim of an outbreak? You little know my people if you think that such would be made without my orders. When the very birds in my dominions would scarcely venture to fly contrary to my will."

Silence fell between the two men. Pizarro was again the outcast, uncomfortable in the presence of royalty. He fiddled with his sword, drew it out of the scabbard, and put it back. The gesture was unconscious, something he often did, but Atahualpa took it as a threat. A shadow passed over his face. At that moment he must have seen a dark gulf opening at his feet.

No more was said. Pizarro went out, taking Little Philip by the hand. At the door the Indian turned and shouted back at the emperor, "You won't live long enough to kill Little Philip. You have a pretty daughter, Inca. But she's not ugly like you. She must be someone else's daughter. Not yours, ugly Inca." He spat at the emperor through the gap in his teeth.

"If Atahualpa does not live long enough to kill you," I said, "and if you ever go near the women again, I'll kill you myself."

Halfway through the door that opened onto the square, Little Philip paused to spit at me. I let him go. I watched the two dodge through the gusts of rain arm in arm and disappear.

I had started after them during a lull in the rain when I caught something on the air that reminded me of a night flower I had once smelled before—was it the scent that Chima had worn? — and I heard close behind me the rustle of a dress. Turning, I saw her standing in the doorway. Her face was pale, almost hidden in a cloud of unkempt hair. She had been crying.

"I listened while you were talking," she said. "I heard my father say that the very birds in his dominions would scarcely venture to fly against his will. It was a boast, and he believes it is true — about the birds and also his people — but deep down in his heart he is afraid. He walks the floor at night. He does not sleep."

I was painfully aware that I had no words to comfort her. I might be able to hide my belief that he was a doomed man. Little else.

"You know Pizarro," she said. "You are friends."

He has no friends, was on my tongue to say. He listens to no one. Not even to God. He pretends to, but he doesn't.

I took her hand, which was cold.

"You know him," she said. "Perhaps you can talk to him about my father and tell Pizarro that he is a good man who is loved by his people. And by me, Chima, his daughter."

"I will talk to Alvarado. He's a friend of your father. And to others. And to . . ." A clap of thunder and a burst of rain scattered my words.

She brushed her hair back from her face. "To the man who dresses in a gown and carries the thing that my father threw in the dirt?"

"To Valverde also."

"And say to him that my father regrets this. My father will not say so, but he does. He has respect for the gods of other people, like the Xiux people who worship the moon. He thinks they are crazy, but he says nothing much and he does not kill them."

She wiped her eyes on the back of her hand. She looked out at me from the big doorway.

"You are standing in the rain," she said.

Suddenly I realized that, yes, I stood in the rain. It was pouring down. It dripped from the peak of my cap and splashed against my legs. The skies had opened up on me.

"You will get drowned soon," she said. "Or get yourself struck upon the head by a lightning bolt. In my country the lightning is fierce. It strikes many people. And they drown many times, too."

"Will you save a drowning man," I said, "who has already been struck by lightning?"

There were only a few short steps to the doorway, between Chima and me. Shyly, she held out her arms.

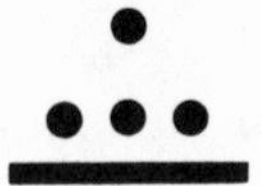

Pizarro gave a fatal twist to the rope he had placed around Atahualpa's neck.

At noon of that day, deeming it wise to have an instant trial and to give it the look of fairness, he called his officers together, appointed from their ranks a prosecutor, a counsel for the prisoner, and two judges.

Atahualpa was charged with the crime of killing his half-brother, Huáscar, with treason against the king of Spain, with having a multitude of wives, with idolatry, with inciting insurrection, and with other dastardly acts — twelve in all.

In a hollow voice Pizarro cautioned everyone against hastiness. Father Valverde swore them to speak the truth on pain of death. Witnesses were called according to the rules of law.

Several Indians, friends of the Inca, testified that he had never plotted against the Spaniards, that he admired them as brave men. But their words, filtered through Little Philip's poisonous tongue, took on a hostile meaning. Soldiers who had stood guard over Atahualpa during his imprisonment swore they had heard him make threats against Pizarro's life. Only four of those in the room objected to the trial. Alvarado rose to say that the Inca should be sent to Spain and tried before the royal *audiencia*. Three of the officers agreed with him.

A secretary carefully took down every word. All the testimony was to be sent to Spain as clear proof to King Carlos that the trial had been conducted under the rules of law.

I expected to testify, since I had done some of the translating between Pizarro and Atahualpa. I was not called. The judges got to their feet. They were filing out to decide on the fate of Atahualpa as I held up my hand and shouted, "Wait!"

Silence fell upon the room that, through the hour the trial lasted, had been loud with chatter, comings and goings. The secretary put aside his pen and began to sharpen another. The judges paused to listen, but Father Valverde herded them outside and slammed the door. He came to where I stood and placed a forefinger on my chest.

"The trial is over," he said.

"I have a statement to make."

"No statements," Valverde said. "The trial is finished."

"Then I'll make a statement to the king."

I asked the secretary, a pale-nosed youth, if he was ready to take down what I was about to say. He sliced on the gray eagle plume, glanced at the officers, then at Pizarro to make sure that they had no objections, then at Father Valverde.

"Statement!" Valverde gasped. "To the king?"

"To the king," I said. "I wish him to know that only one crime was committed and that it was not committed by Atahualpa."

Valverde wagged his scanty locks. "Nonsense," he cried.

The secretary put down his pen.

Valverde was still close to me, his forefinger pressing on my chest. He came closer and spoke in a whisper.

"The ring you wear," he said, "the bishop's ring you have there on your finger. How did you come by it?"

I was not taken aback by his question. From the hour we had met, not a day went by that I hadn't looked for it.

"Dicing," I said.

"With whom?"

"A professional gambler. A very clever gentleman."

"When?"

"Years ago, Father, in my early youth. When I was a gambler myself."

"You are still a gambler," Valverde said. "You gamble now. And with another experienced gambler. But now you dice for higher stakes. Your life, my friend, your life!"

While we glared at each other, the judges, gone scarcely long enough to be seated, filed back. They brought with them a verdict of guilty on all counts and the suggestion that Atahualpa be burned at the stake before the day came to an end.

The emperor was taken back to his quarters. Soon afterward, on the pretense that I was carrying a message from Valverde, I slipped past the guards. I found Atahualpa on his knees, gazing at a set of blue stone pebbles he had arranged in an odd pattern on the floor.

"Inca Capac," I said, "listen closely."

The emperor did not look up, but kept his gaze fixed on the blue stones.

"When you leave this room, turn to the right and follow the passage beyond the main gate that is guarded. There are three turnings — as you know — all toward your right hand. This passage leads to the women's quarters. Yesterday I saw this passage, just as I have described it to you. Once you are with the women, they will find a place to hide you. By tomorrow or the day following, I'll find you a means of escape."

It was a desperate chance.

Atahualpa said nothing. He shifted the stones around to a different pattern. Then he glanced up at me and said, "The blue stones speak the end of my days."

In his eyes I saw the same veiled look I had seen in the eyes of Moctezuma on the day Cortés condemned him to death — the same Indian look of resignation. Without further words I left him.

Two hours after sunset, by torchlight, the Spanish army assembled in the great square. Atahualpa was led out by Father

Valverde. It had begun to rain. The faggots collected for the fire burned slowly.

The emperor was bound to a stake and the fire pushed closer. He glanced at those gathered around him, at Pizarro and Vincente de Valverde, at the dark sky. He closed his eyes then and stood in a trance.

Father Valverde spoke to him through the small voice of Little Philip, saying that if he would renounce the faith of his fathers and become a Christian, he would be spared the tortures of the fire that burned beside him and those of everlasting hell.

Atahualpa mumbled a reply — a few words that Little Philip embroidered at such length that I couldn't make head or tail of them. Valverde, taking it as a sign that the Inca had embraced the faith, ordered his fate changed from death by burning to the more merciful death of strangulation.

Valverde raised an ebony cross and in a soft voice gave the emperor the new name of Juan de Atahualpa. A stout rope was placed about his neck.

I was standing beside Pizarro, facing him in fact. I saw him watch closely as the rope was looped in back and a stick inserted in the loop and turned by two stout men.

His expression didn't change until the stick would not turn and he saw that the emperor no longer breathed. Then he raised his eyes to the sunless heavens, and there came over his face a look of utter bliss. The one man he envied, whose power he craved, whose courage outmatched his own, was dead. Francisco Pizarro — the bastard pig boy from the alleys of Seville, now Inca Pizarro, King of the Four Quarters, Lord of the Sharp Knives? Anything was possible in the land of Peru. He fell to his knees and, between quiet sobs, prayed.

The officers prayed, too, and all the soldiers, thankful that a great danger had been lifted from their lives.

No sounds came from the quarters where the women were

watching, only a deep silence. But the next day, when the emperor's body was placed in the church, the women and children and servants burst forth, streaming across the square in a black tide.

They were halted at the church doors by Father Valverde, who explained that since the emperor had died in the Christian faith, a Christian service was being held, and they could not enter. The women brushed him aside, broke through the door, and surged down the aisle, crying out that they wished to join the Inca in death.

I was standing next to the old noble, caretaker of the Inca's pleasure-house, when the tide of mourners swept down the aisle. Chima and her mother came last, walking slowly by themselves — two proud women, their eyes red from weeping.

Chima glanced at me and quickly turned away. But in that brief moment, stronger than any words, I saw in her eyes a look of dread and distrust, a nameless horror of all those who had invaded her home, killed the Inca people, and betrayed her father. It was an accusing look that struck deep into my heart.

Soldiers herded the women through the rain back to their quarters. I went there to find Chima but was turned away by Pizarro's guards. At dawn, when I went again, I learned that she had fled from Cajamarca, borne away by servants who feared for her safety. I also learned that her mother had taken her own life in sorrow over the emperor's death, as had many of the women.

The next morning de Soto returned from Guamachucho. Appalled to hear that the emperor was dead, he sought out Pizarro and found him at the church, sitting beside the door, attired in mourning black with his great felt hat slouched over his eyes, for all to witness the depth of his sorrow.

De Soto was not taken in. He told Pizarro that the execution of Atahualpa was a rash and unnecessary act. On his journey to Guamachucho and in the city itself, he had met with nothing save friendship. At once Pizarro placed the blame on others, especially upon Vincente de Valverde. With cold ferocity, Valverde then turned on Pizarro.

After two days of violent argument, when his rage still had not cooled, Valverde turned on me. I was detained, placed in Atahualpa's old quarters, and charged with the murder of Bishop Pedroza. His evidence was flimsy, mere hearsay, but next to Pizarro his word was supreme. It would be easy for him to have me tried. Few would come forward in my behalf, for I had lost favor with Pizarro.

He would have tried me at once except for the excitement caused among the soldiery by Atahualpa's death. The streets of Cajamarca rang with triumphant shouts. The road to Cuzco, the fabulous city, was finally open!

At the height of the excitement, during the last hours of wild preparations for the march on Cuzco, bribing a guard with half the gold I owned, I rode out of the city on a windy morning just before daylight. I rode straight to the emperor's pleasure-house, where I learned that Chima had stopped for only a night, then fled on to Abancay, a secluded village near Cuzco.

I hid in the pleasure-house. I could not continue on the road that Pizarro and Valverde would take. A conspicuous figure — a tall Spaniard with sun-bleached hair riding a dappled horse — would surely be reported.

The old noble showed me a large *sala* of marble and precious woods, but I chose a small room at the back of the palace that had been Chima's playroom when she was a child. The Spaniards had rooted it upside down searching for gold, but her couch was there and childish designs she apparently had stitched and hung on the walls.

It was strange being in her room, like nothing that had ever happened to me in my life . . . Things about Chima that I hadn't noticed before — the first day we met and later when I stood in the rain and gave her my rosary — all this I suddenly remembered.

In the beginning I hadn't thought of her beauty. But now, as she walked gracefully before me in memory, her thin shoulders thrown back as though she carried a light burden on her head, her dark eyes rayed with flecks of amber, I was stunned with her beauty.

Now, as I gazed at the sky, the road that wound through the shadowy hills, the sparkling leaves of the tree beside the window, everything I saw looked different. I forgot the awful truth that Chima had fled from me, no less than from Pizarro.

I stayed in hiding for nine long days, until he and his army had gone by. I then took the road to Abancay.

For a week I rode close behind the army — at times in its dust. Soon afterward, my mare wore her shoes so thin that I was forced to stop in the town of Xauxa to have her reshod.

Pizarro had just left. He had encountered trouble in this town, caused, he believed, by an Indian cacique who was serving the army as a guide. The cacique was accused of sending secret messages to Quizquiz, a powerful chief who was waiting near Cuzco to attack the Spaniards. The cacique was converted to Christianity by Valverde, then burned at the stake. His body, surrounded by a flock of carrion birds, lay in the town square when I arrived.

I found the natives subdued and fearful, yet friendly. They knew nothing about horseshoes, of course, but I was sent to a metal worker, who took patterns and, mixing the soft gold I gave him with a hard alloy, made four serviceable shoes. They lasted for several months, through bad country, in rain and sleet and snow.

I caught up with the army at Xaquixaguana, a village five leagues from Cuzco. I found a place to stay on its outskirts with a farmer and his wife. From them I learned that a girl had passed through the village some weeks before, borne in a litter by eight young nobles. The litter, they said, carried the royal mark of Inca Atahualpa.

I stayed on with the family after Pizarro moved his army

to Cuzco. Manco, the farmer, went to market there with his produce twice each week and came back with news of the Spaniards. They were rifling the palaces, stripping gold plates from the walls and arcades, digging up streets and gardens for treasures they thought had been buried, invading the temples. They raped the women who had not fled.

To my great distress, Manco brought from Cuzco not a word, not so much as a rumor, about Chima Atahualpa. The girl had disappeared.

Then, suddenly, Pizarro moved out of Cuzco for the coast, taking with him Father Valverde and all of his army except a small garrison of forty, which he left to guard the city. The day I heard of his departure I started for Cuzco.

Cuzco is a cloud city, high among the Andes Mountains, more than two leagues above the level of the sea. By now winter had set in, and a cold wind was sweeping down from the snowy peaks. As I descended upon it from a narrow pass, I saw destruction on every side. Some of the buildings had furnishings piled in front of them, others were in ashes. On the main square, what must have been Atahualpa's palace showed gaping holes where gold plates and decorations had been torn away.

Having nothing to fear from the garrison Pizarro had left behind, some of whom were my friends, I went first to them to ask about Chima. I found a dispirited bunch. Now that the city had been sacked, they had nothing to do. The gold bars they had received in Cajamarca were tightly sewn into their jackets and they slept with one eye open.

Nobody had seen or heard news of Chima Atahualpa. It was suggested that she might have gone to Quito, where her father had been born and where he wished to be buried. But Quito was far to the north in the opposite direction. Manco and his wife had definitely seen her on the road to Cuzco. The officer in charge of the garrison suggested that I visit the convent on the opposite side of the square.

After prolonged knocking at the convent's battered gate, I heard a fearful voice ask my business. I described it and received the answer that Chima Atahualpa had taken refuge there before the Spaniards came, but had fled.

"Fled where?" I asked.

"Far off," the woman said.

"To another convent?"

There was silence and I repeated the question. The woman would not answer.

"I have words for her," I said. "It is necessary that she hear them."

"Give the words to me," she said. "I will see that she hears them. We send words."

"I have important words for her ears," I said, realizing that there was no written Inca language. "It is necessary that she hear them."

"Give me the words," the woman said, "and the Sweet Child of the Sun will hear them."

What could I say? What message could I possibly send to Chima that wouldn't make me out to be a lovesick fool? There was nothing, nothing!

"I will take the words myself. They are necessary. They are from her mother," I suddenly decided to say. "Where do I go? In what direction? What is the name of this place, tell me!"

"You cannot go," the woman said. "It is forbidden."

"Someone must go or else the messages cannot be delivered. Who does go?"

"Girls and women go."

"When?"

"During the nights of the dark moon."

"Only then?"

She did not answer. I heard footsteps moving away, the closing of a heavy door.

That day I took up quarters in a building the Spaniards had sacked. From the roof I had a clear view of the convent and its only gate. On the sixth night of my vigil, soon after dusk, a litter borne by six women came out of the gate, circled the square, and struck out to the north on a trail I had crossed when entering Cuzco.

I followed them at a safe distance. When they camped near midnight, in a thatched hut beside the river, I camped also, well out of sight. I slept little, bothered by the horrible suspicion that the woman at the gate had lied to me and that at the very moment we were talking, Chima was hidden away somewhere in the convent.

We followed the river for two days, moving down through a canyon shadowed by towering cliffs. On the third day we crossed the river on an osier bridge and started upward on a trail into the heart of the mountains, among peaks sparkling with snow. I say "we," though at no time did I meet the bearers.

We climbed all that day and stopped often, for the air was thin and hard to breathe. I walked part of the time to rest my horse. We reached the snow line toward evening. From there the trail ran level, teetering on the edge of an abyss. The sun on the snow was blinding.

For an hour or less we traveled along a narrow shelf of rock, steep on both sides, and then came upon a stone wall that ran in a curved line for half a league, from one abyss to another, blocking our way.

The wall was thrice my height as I sat in the saddle, too high to climb. But it was not its height that astounded me. The wall was made of huge stones — many of them fifty or sixty feet in circumference. And what was truly remarkable, they were fitted edge to edge, beveled so tight together that they looked to be the work of a lapidary, not a mason but someone who engraved precious stones.

The trail led to a massive gate, pierced by a smaller gate at which stood two tall men in black robes. The litter came to a halt and a brief conversation took place. Then the smaller gate was opened and the litter passed through. Before the gate closed, the bearers — all armed with clubs — glanced back at me.

Apparently, the two guards had never seen a horse or imagined one. Their first impulse, I am sure, was to flee, but they stood their ground and, though trembling, barred my way with crossed spears. They said nothing. They looked at the sky and not at me, standing fixed as if they meant to stay there forever.

"I have come here to see Atahualpa Capac's daughter," I said.

There was no response from either of the Indians, who looked alike and could have been brothers — two brown statues with blank faces. A third Indian came from somewhere and stood beside the two silent ones. He was small and wore in his ears big gold loops that rested on his shoulders.

"I bring an urgent message," I said. "It is from the mother of Atahualpa's daughter."

"Which daughter?" the noble said. "Atahualpa has many daughters. Three of them are here now in our city of Machu Picchu."

"Her name is Chima. I have come from Cuzco with . . ."

"There is only one road to Machu Picchu," the nobleman said, "and it comes only from Cuzco. We have seen you coming each day from Cuzco. You sometimes talk to someone, yet you are alone. It is odd. Perhaps you talk to the beast. You walk sometimes also instead of sitting in comfort on your beast like the other Spaniards. Odd. Would you like a drink? You pant like a dog. There is little air here among the clouds. What drink would you like, tall young fellow?"

"Water," I said. "Cold if you have it."

I noticed that he was wearing Spanish boots. They were a trifle large for him, but polished to a nice shine. Somewhere, probably in Cuzco, he had encountered Pizarro's army.

The water came ice-cold in a golden cup. When I had drunk my fill and water had been brought to my horse — tubs of water — the noble opened the small gate and stood aside for me to pass.

He led me down a path paved with marble and through a garden where all the flowers were gold, so delicately made that they moved in the light wind. Among the flowers were golden butterflies and golden birds with ruby eyes. It was an amazing sight. Clearly, no Spaniard had ever set foot here.

At the far end of the garden stood a pleasure-palace, like Atahualpa's palace at Cajamarca, though smaller. After I had tied my horse, I was led down a dim hall into a room lit by candles, whose walls were stark white. In a far corner sat a woman dressed in a shimmering red gown that clung to her body. Her bare feet rested on a cushion.

The little man gave me a name that he must have made up and the woman a name of many syllables I didn't catch. In time, I called her Magdalena.

"She is the priestess of the temple," he said, "where Chima Atahualpa now lives. She will listen to the message you have brought and decide if the emperor's daughter should hear it."

The little man slipped away, his army boots soundless on the stone floor. The woman was silent. Whether she knew that I was in the room I could not tell.

"I have come a long way to bring this message for Chima Atahualpa," I said, out of breath and impatient.

I waited for an answer. She was chewing on a little red nut, or rather rolling it around on her tongue. It had stained her lips red and moistened them so that they glistened in the candlelight.

"It is a long journey," she said at last in a throaty voice barely loud enough to hear. "Returning will be even longer, or so our pilgrims complain."

She crossed her feet, and I noticed that the nails were tinted the same color as her mouth.

"The message is from Chima's mother? That's curious, because she is not alive," the priestess said. Then, perhaps to soften my embarrassment at being caught in a lie, she added, "The dead often send messages. And they are always important. What message do *you* bring from her mother? Tell me, so that it can be delivered at once. The dead are not impatient, but they wield power. It is wise to humor them."

With a click of a fingernail she summoned a servant, whispered in his ear, and sent him away. She glanced at me, waiting for a reply. Her eyes were black and the lids painted with blue shadows.

When I fumbled at an answer, she said, "Chima Atahualpa has taken the vows of chastity. She is now a Virgin of the Sun."

The words sank into my flesh like the coldest steel. I was too stunned to speak.

"She is a mere child," the priestess said. "Pretty, loving, but a child. Set your mind to rest. Forget the Princess Atahualpa."

I managed to speak. "You ask something of me that I cannot do."

"You must," the priestess said. "There is no other way. A vow was taken. Nothing can break it."

She got to her feet and led me from the room onto a balcony that seemed to hang in midair. It was evening now, and a purple haze covered the snowy peaks. Far below, in a small pocket between the peaks, the haze was deeper, yet scattered lights were beginning to show.

"You are looking down upon the village of Machu Picchu," the priestess said. "The cluster of lights you see there at the center is the Temple of the Sun. It is where Chima lives and hundreds of other virgins live. Their lives are dedicated to the sun. To the sun alone. Look once and for the last time.

Then close your eyes and close your mind to what is forbidden. She is safe in the Temple of the Sun."

I looked down through the darkening haze at the clustered lights — one quick glance — and turned away. The last of the evening glow rested for a moment on the woman's face. She was neither old nor young. She once had been beautiful.

Palatial quarters were prepared for me, far more luxurious than those I had enjoyed as Kukulcán, Lord of the Evening Star. I dined alone that night on sumptuous fare and lay down in a bed wide enough for half a dozen men, under blankets of the finest llama wool. I should have slept well, exhausted as I was by the arduous climb, yet I scarcely closed my eyes.

I had only the woman's word that Chima had made vows that bound her to the sun god. It was possible that she was only a student, as I once had been, a beginner learning the rites of worship. But how was I to know this, except by talking to her? I had been forbidden to see her — not threatened, but warned. The palace was surrounded by guards. I had seen them patrolling the wall when I came in. Indeed, as an intruder and a Spaniard, I was actually in danger of my life.

Snow fell in the night, large flakes like feathers settling over the village, so that at dawn, when I looked down upon it from my window, I was unable to make out even the faintest lines of the temple. Everything was lost in a field of glistening white.

I saw nothing of the priestess that day, though once in the evening I heard her give instructions in her throaty voice to the little nobleman. What they were I couldn't tell. I was fed three bountiful meals and in between was brought trays of prickly tuna fruit and green-fleshed pears, though it was not the season for fruit.

Toward dusk of the following day I was visited by two female servants, who removed the rough clothes I wore and dressed me in a flowing tunic, sandals tasseled with gold flowers, and a cap of wool and feathers. Everything fit me so perfectly that it appeared someone had taken my old clothes while I slept and modeled new ones from them. But, surveying myself in a copper shield that the servants held up, I had a moment of panic. The man who gazed back at me was Kukulcán, Lord of the Four Winds. I turned away.

That evening the priestess was waiting in a different room from the one where she had received me before. It had no windows, but the ceiling, thanks to an arrangement of gold baffles that slid back and forth, lay open to the sky.

She sat on a low bench encrusted with jewels, shading her face against the westering sun. At her feet a sleeping pink-skinned dog, one of the hairless breed, raised its head, sniffed, and went back to sleep. Her jeweled hands cast a shadow that concealed her eyes, but certainly she was carefully studying me.

After a long silence, she said, "You are not an Inca nor a Maya nor an Aztecatl. Not with this blue gaze and this corn-colored hair. You must belong to those who destroyed our beautiful city of Cuzco. You are one of those who call themselves Spaniards, yes? But you do not look like the ones who came here among the peaks and knocked at our gates. I only saw these men when they were dead, lying on the ground, dead. But they were very small, all seven of them. Small and dark, not like you. You are different. You are not a real Spaniard."

I smiled and thanked her, but I was not deceived. Beneath the honeyed words I heard a bitter strain of hatred.

She picked up the hairless dog and kissed it. "Your thoughts are troubled," she said. "You brood about the princess."

The priestess turned her head and gave me a sidelong glance. "My heart goes out to you," she said. "I have been in love myself long ago. I am familiar with the pangs you suffer, the sleepless nights and clouded days — all this I know."

She fell silent for a while, then called the old noble and instructed him to send word to the temple and let the girl know that I was here on the mountaintop, waiting to talk to her.

The instructions were clear, the old noble carefully repeated them — he seemed somewhat deaf — but when I went back to my quarters a short time later and looked down at the road that led to the temple, I saw that the snow that covered it lay level and unmarked.

No one went to the temple the next day — I watched the road for hours — nor the day following. Then it snowed again, and when I asked the priestess to let me take my horse and ride to the temple, she refused me.

"Men are forbidden in the temple," she said. "Those who dare to go there never come back. The snow will melt soon, and on that day I will send a swift messenger."

Days went by, a week, a month. Then a warm wind came up the slopes from somewhere and in hours melted the snow that covered the road. At once a messenger ran to the temple and returned to say that the temple was closed and solemn rites were being held, which would last for another quarter of the moon.

At the end of this time the messenger sped down again, was gone for two days, and then came back, bringing an answer from Chima Atahualpa. It was not a spoken answer. The messenger handed me a small package sealed with wax.

I was eating dinner. Leaving the table, I went to the window, where the light was better, and opened the package with trembling hands. A sheaf of dried leaves taken from a *dama de la noche* vine was wrapped around a string of beads and a crucifix. It was the rosary I had given Chima in Cajamarca months before.

From the moment I first learned that she had sealed herself

off in the Temple of the Sun, I had thought the act was caused by the tragedies that had befallen her. She would return to the world. But now, stronger than any words, the rosary was a message of renunciation.

I barred the door and stood at the window looking down upon the temple. I stood there until night fell across the peaks of Machu Picchu and hid the temple from my sight. The priestess, alarmed when I did not appear that evening or the next day, sent the old noble in his creaking Spanish boots to see if I were still alive. I sent him off with a curse upon him and his family.

When I did appear, some three days later, the priestess was shocked at my appearance.

"You alarm me," she said. "You are like a dead man who turns his back upon the grave and tries to walk away. Come and sit here and let me comfort you with my thoughts."

I wanted none of her comforting thoughts. Nothing except to leave Machu Picchu. I told her so with what politeness I could summon. She called the old noble and he came tripping in with his catbird walk — five quick hops and then a pause.

"You remember," he said when I asked him for my horse, "that we sent the animal to the lowlands because we had no food for it here in the snow."

I didn't remember. My memory, always good, had begun to fail me. "Bring the horse," I said. "To save time, have someone ride her back."

Men were sent down the mountain. They returned without the horse. The osier bridge had been ripped from its moorings by a storm, and the river could not be crossed.

I considered crossing the river on foot, but was warned that it would mean my death. At this moment I began to feel that I would never see the horse again. Nor would I be allowed to leave the mountain. I was a prisoner. Machu Picchu was a jail. The priestess, I realized, was my jailer.

She was very understanding after that, and while I was waiting for the bridge to be built again, every night I was invited to have dinner with her. She wanted to know about the land I came from and what gods I worshipped there. She wondered if all the men were as tall as I was and were blond. She loved my hair when the candlelight shone on it, and once made up a little poem about it and sang it in her throaty voice.

She talked a lot, but not about her own life. About herself she was quiet, but I gained the impression that she was a woman of high birth. She even hinted very delicately that she had once been in love with Atahualpa Capac himself and he with her. But it was a different man — his cousin? — whom she had really loved and loved now.

The night she hinted at all this we fell to talking about love, about Chima — she spoke of her as a spoiled child who didn't know her own mind — and, still talking about love, she took my hand in hers, gently as if it were some precious ornament.

Never before, since the day I arrived at the palace, had I heard a note of music, but now suddenly it seemed to come from everywhere. A musician in a room far off would play a piece and no sooner finish than another would take up the same strain on a different instrument from a different room — a strange, unfamiliar music of tinkling stops and starts played in a minor key.

Her mouth was now close to mine, so near that our breaths mingled. She laid my hand on her bodice, and then on one soft breast.

I was embarrassed, terribly so, yet she was not discouraged. Nor was she repelled by my awkwardness. In fact, dropping her gown to the floor, she reveled in my youthful dismay as I saw for the first time a woman's body in all its majesty.

The night was brief, and when gray dawn stood at the windows and the snowy peaks of Machu Picchu showed pink against the sky, the morning stole upon me as a surprise.

RETA E. KING LIBRARY
CHADRON STATE COLLEGE
CHADRON, NE 69337

They became an addiction, an overpowering drug, these nights. I lived for them. They were never out of my waking thoughts. At times, frightened by the power she held over me, I prayed to God for deliverance. Truthfully, I tried to pray and failed. The words never left my mouth.

Spring brought an end to this madness. It came suddenly on a bright noon when the old nobleman appeared while the priestess and I were eating breakfast. He turned his back to me, whispered a name in her ear, and left. In a few minutes he returned with a handsome Indian dressed in the regalia of an Inca noble. I was aware at once, as a secret look passed between them, that this was the man the priestess loved.

They brought my horse up from the lowlands late that day. I bade farewell to the priestess with a show of courtesy that I did not feel, no longer bewitched by her storm of black hair and her cinnamon-colored skin.

I rode away at a walk, unnoticed. Instead of taking the road that led out of Machu Picchu, on an overpowering impulse I rode down the slope to the Temple of the Sun.

The massive, gold-studded door was open and women were standing about, their arms full of flowers. They scattered at my approach and I rode through the doorway into a vaulted room, toward the sound of young voices singing in unison, past a gigantic gold replica of the sun, lit by votive candles.

The virgins, clad all in white, quit singing and scurried back into the shadows. All save one, who stood facing me as I reined the horse toward her. She wore a dress of springtime colors, her hair caught up in a band of golden beads.

"I have come to take you away, Chima."

Frightened murmurs from the girls who had hidden drowned out my words. I spoke again. Chima did not answer.

"You returned the rosary given to you in Cajamarca," I said. "And for a long time I thought you had returned it because you blamed me for your father's death."

"You were to blame. And you are to blame now."

"I did all that I could to save him, before the trial and while it was taking place. After the trial I went to see your father and planned a way for him to escape."

"A dozen guards were watching. How could he ever escape?"

"There was a chance."

"A chance for you to win favors from him?" Chima said.

"A man sentenced to death doesn't have favors to give," I said. "But we talk words. Words mean nothing."

"The words of a Spaniard mean nothing," she said.

There were cries now in the street. Voices came from the doorway. I slid down from the horse and went toward her. She retreated from my outstretched hand. In desperation I grasped her arm. She pulled away.

Light from the votive candles fell upon her face, and I saw then the same look of horror and distrust that I had seen when she walked down the aisle to her father's bier.

She was moving away from me. The mammoth gold image of the sun, blindingly bright, now stood between us. From far off came the sound of girls softly chanting.

Chima had gone into the shadow of the sun's image. She had disappeared. I called her name. There was no answer, only the sound of running steps.

Dazed, I rode out of the temple, scattering a crowd of women who pelted me with stones and curses. Screams followed me up the winding street. By the time I reached the summit and the great wall loomed before me, all sounds had died away in icy silence.

Guards were lounging at the gate as I suddenly appeared before them, not fifty paces away. Taken by surprise, they did not move. Then two of the men recovered themselves and ran to close me off.

I slashed them aside and spurred my horse through the narrow opening. A cluster of stone huts barred the way, and as I chose a path around them, one of the guards overtook me and grasped the horse's tail. I dragged him for a distance, bumping over the rocks, until he finally fell behind.

I rode all that night, still in a daze. I reached Cuzco at sundown and fell asleep in a gutted temple, slept till noon of the following day, and, avoiding Pizarro's garrison, rode out of the city.

I stayed with Manco the farmer, recovering my strength. I learned that Pizarro had struck out for the coast, and that he and Alvarado had become enemies, that ambitious Captain Almagro had sworn to kill Pizarro. The soldiers, as usual, were interested not in killing each other but in gold, which they sat through the nights gambling away. Recovered from the first shock of the Spanish onslaught, the Indians were gathering in mountain villages, arming themselves against the hour when they could slay their tormentors.

I caught up with Captain Alvarado and served him indifferently until the day we reached the sea, where I left him. When I had thoughts, which was seldom, they were confused. One scene faded into another as in a nightmare — the *Santa Margarita* lying wrecked on a hidden reef; Julián Escobar, seminarian, before the godhouse, blood running around my feet, speaking as a god to the multitude, at Moctezuma's side while he read his fate in a bird that talked; Pedroza's eyes when he ignored the obsidian knife poised above him; Atahualpa, last of the Incas, at the hour of his betrayal and death — all, even the memory of my beloved Chima, everything pointless, confused, and time distorted as in a frightful dream.

In San Miguel I boarded a ship for the port of Panamá, using up the last of the gold I had saved. In time I sold my horse and her gold horseshoes to a young man on his way to Peru, and with the money bought passage to Spain.

After an accident to the ship's rudder in a violent storm that sent us into the Azores for a month of repairs, I arrived safely at the mouth of the Guadalquivir. We made good time against the flooding river and docked in Seville on a feast day.

The city was brimming with joy. Church bells rang the hours and the quarters between. Flags flew from the *embarcadero,* from the Tower of Gold, and from the ships along the river.

By chance, as I went ashore I noticed that the caravel moored at our stern carried the name *Santa Margarita.*

I shouted to a sinewy man leaning against the ship's rail, "Does this belong to Guillermo Cantú, the dwarf?"

"It does," the sailor shouted back, "if you refer to Cantú, the Marquis of Santa Cruz and the Seven Cities."

I was somewhat abashed by the dwarf's new, resounding

title, for I hadn't thought of him in years and I had no urge to see him now. Out of curiosity I asked the sailor if the marquis was on board.

He pointed across the river. "The church over there? Near it, a tower?"

I looked and saw a tower almost as tall as the Giralda.

"That's where the marquis lives when he's here in Seville. Mostly he lives in Madrid."

"Where's the Marquis of Santa Cruz now?"

"Here. At the *feria*."

"Feria?"

"The fiesta. You never heard of it? You must have been gone a long time."

"I have."

"A grand fiesta," the sailor said. "Dancing. Processions, Firecrackers. The *ricos* have booths and they entertain friends. Every year they have the *feria,* now that the treasure fleets come regularly. It goes on night and day. You're just in time for the festivities."

At my lack of enthusiasm, the sailor grew suspicious, mumbled something, and walked away — he might, by chance, be talking to a heretic.

Before I had climbed up from the river four boys, mistaking me for a conquistador, fastened themselves upon me — one at the rear, one on each side, and one in front, walking backward. They wanted gold. I turned my pockets inside out, hoping to drive them off.

"What's in the sack?" the pimply youth in the rear wanted to know.

"Nothing you'll like," I said, opening the sack.

They all glanced in. One of them said, "Nothing. He hasn't been anywhere."

"He's been down the river fishing," another said. "And caught nothing. No wonder he's got a long horse face."

I lost them in the crowd of revelers.

Both sides of the street that led to the cathedral were lined by cloth pavilions decked with flowers and ribbons and gaudy signs of welcome, belonging apparently to the *ricos* the sailor had mentioned. I recognized none of them or members of their families, but I had not gone far when my name was called out from one of the pavilions.

Guillermo Cantú made his way through a swarm of pretty girls. At first I thought that by some miracle he had grown — he now reached to my shoulder. I saw then that he was wearing gold, stiltlike extensions on his legs and high gold boots. His face had not changed. He still had the twisted little smile and the darting gleam in his eyes. It was, indeed, my old friend the dwarf.

He clasped me in a boisterous *embrazo*. A servant put a glass of *manzanilla* in my hand. The pretty girls, who were half his age and mine, when told by Cantú that I had once been Emperor of the Maya, giggled and pressed themselves upon me, clamoring to hear about my kingdom.

"Don Julián Escobar, you come at a lucky time," he said. "One of my fleets is due in any day. I'll make you my commodore. You'll never need to leave Seville. You'll inspect the ships — there are ten in a flotilla, and I have two flotillas. You'll see that the ships are in condition and properly provisioned."

He threw his arms about me again, overjoyed with the wonderful prospects. For a moment I thought that he might go into his little dance; then he grew sober and tried to explain why, at the hour of danger, when I was in dire need of the *Santa Margarita,* he had turned tail and sailed off for Spain.

I didn't bother to listen. Uneasily, he got around to the subject of gold — the amount he had carried off and the rightful share that belonged to me.

"The Governor of Hispaniola took a nibble," he said. "King

Carlos took a bite." He pointed to a man sitting in one of the pavilions. "That's Don Andrés, the chief officer of the House of Contracts. You can't sail out of the harbor without his consent. Don Andrés took not a bite but a mouthful."

A tear showed in one of his eyes. He groaned.

"There was little left," he said with a sigh. "A pittance."

"More gold than that, Don Guillermo. You can't make soup out of stones, as the saying goes, nor can you build a fleet of ships out of a pittance."

He studied me. "Four thousand gold pesos?" he said.

A fortune, but the thought of so much gold did not lift my spirits. Truthfully, the thought was distasteful.

"Five thousand," he said, taking my silence for disappointment.

"Double the amount," I said, as I saw a line of ragged figures approach us.

"Agreed," he said gaily, delighted that I hadn't demanded more. "Come tomorrow and I'll have it for you."

The chattering girls were suddenly quiet. The revelers who choked the aisle between the pavilions drew aside to let the figures pass. They carried candles and were dressed in black gowns and black hoods that hid their faces. I recognized them as members of a lay brotherhood whose lives were dedicated to the poor.

"Tomorrow, when you come," I said on an impulse that I could not explain, "when you bring my share of the gold, give it to these gentlemen."

The Marquis of Santa Cruz was startled. He had thoughts of backing out of the bargain.

"Little good it will do," he said.

"It belongs to the Brothers of the Poor," I said, as I walked away. "See that they receive it, every peso. If you fail, you'll hear from me, Cantú."

"If it serves to lighten your conscience, Lord Kukulcán," the dwarf called after me. "You always had a heavy one."

I did not answer. I left the street of pavilions. The sound of guitars and laughter faded away. A cluster of women sat beside the cathedral door, some with children, all pale, their hands held out for alms.

I went down the long dark aisle to a chapel where I had often prayed before. I knelt in a corner, away from the light of votive candles. The marble floor was cold. I clasped my hands and gazed up at the Virgin above the altar in her white robes. Around her neck were coils of gold, and on her fingers sparkling rings that must have come from the New World, for I had never seen them before.

But as I gazed, slowly her face disappeared. Instead, I saw the great gold image in the Temple of the Sun. Then Chima's face — all innocence and beauty. Then this changed and the priestess was looking down at me, as her raven locks took on the shape of writhing serpents.

In panic I sought a chapel where no candles burned. It belonged to wise St. Augustine, Bishop of Hippo. I got to my knees and gazed up at his painting. In the darkness it, too, slowly changed and showed no longer St. Augustine but a portrait of Bishop Pedroza as he lay on the sacrificial stone, the obsidian knife poised above his breast.

I hurried away. At the cathedral door I stopped suddenly, as if an iron fist had grasped me.

Beside the curtained door that shut out the church from the sounds of revelry was an alms box and an old woman on guard, sitting behind it asleep. In one painful moment, I wrenched the amethyst ring from my finger and pushed it through the slot. I heard a small tinkling sound as it struck copper coins on the bottom of the box. The old woman opened her eyes and blessed me.

I stood in the darkness looking down at her. You do not understand, old woman, I said to myself. I had the power to save Pedroza, but I let him die. He died because I could not live in peace knowing that he held power over me and something that I coveted. I was like Pizarro, the pig boy, who coveted the power of Atahualpa. No, giving this amethyst ring to the poor does not absolve me of the crime. Nor does the gift of gold I have made. I must seek it in some other way, old woman. But how? In some other place, old woman who blesses me. But where?

I went out into the April sun and chose the road toward Arroyo. Near the top of the first hill, the stagecoach overtook me. It was the old one I had ridden in before, many times, only now it was painted blue and yellow and red for the fiesta and had a young driver I hadn't seen before. He cracked his whip and drove on when he learned that I was penniless.

Don Alfredo Luz, the *alcalde* of Arroyo, riding a sleek gray horse with his wife on a pillion behind him, came up the far side of the hill. In my present condition, having no desire to talk, I glanced about for a place to hide. The hill was without tree or bush. I stood in the middle of the road and greeted them with a stiff bow.

"Welcome, señor," Don Alfredo said. "You have been away a very long time. Welcome, welcome! We've heard so many things, we scarcely know what to believe. We heard you were with Hernán Cortés. Then it was Francisco Pizarro."

Doña Elena, his wife, said, "Then Magellan and you sailed around the world. Is that true? Is the world really round?" She paused. "Your mother died of pains in her chest, did you know?"

"No, I didn't," I said without emotion. Now at least my mother wouldn't be disappointed because I was not yet a bishop, let alone a priest — that I had come home from the golden cities empty-handed.

"Your sister is married and has two children," Doña Elena said. "The boy looks like you."

"I guess it doesn't make much difference about the world," the *alcalde* said, "whether it's round or flat."

"Other things," I said, "are more important."

"You've seen so many sights in your wanderings," Doña Elena said from her soft perch behind her husband, "do tell us about them sometime."

"Round or flat, the world's far bigger these days," Don Alfredo said, "since Magellan and Pizarro and Cortés have been nosing about."

"And so full of wonders," his wife said.

"It's not only the world that's full of wonders," I said. "Life is full of wonders, too, monstrous wonders!"

My words were lost on Doña Elena.

"Yes," she said. "When Captain Pizarro came asking for money — three years ago, was it not, Don Alfredo?" The *alcalde* thought it was three. "Anyway, he brought a band of Indians with him to show everyone. You should have seen them. All decked out in feathers and swirly tattoos and big round rings in their ears. The men, that is. The women had hair they covered with some kind of purple grease, and it hung down below their waists. And they wore bells on their bare ankles."

"And millions of them out there in Spain's new world," Don Alfredo said. "Little wonder that Pizarro has such a time trying to save souls."

"Honestly, Julián, do you think that these heathens *have* souls?" Doña Elena asked me.

"Yes, souls," I said. "Also, the men bleed when wounded and the women weep in sorrow."

Don Alfredo was suddenly uncomfortable, as the sailor on the banks of the Guadalquivir had been uncomfortable. He turned his horse in a circle and Doña Elena raised her pink parasol.

"Are you returning to your studies?" she said.

I shook my head. "I have come to doubt that I've been called to speak for Christ."

"What a shame, Julián. You would make such an excellent priest — so sympathetic and kind and thoughtful of other people. Oh, my!"

"If I can be of help to you," Don Alfredo said.

"Yes, if we can," Doña Elena said.

I thanked the *alcalde* and his wife and they did not detain me further. Waving their gloved hands, they rode down the sunny trail toward the fair.

At the bottom of the next hill stood the gray stone dwelling that housed the Brothers of the Poor. It was off the trail in a meadow beside a stream. I had never talked to any of the brothers, though I had seen them working in their scanty fields in black gowns and cowls. They were a clannish lot, having little to do with anyone who wasn't poor.

I went down a path overgrown with weeds that led to the door of their dwelling. Carved above the door, in the stone lintel, was a legend. I tried to make out the letters, but all that I could see was "Anno MCCCLX" and the words "Know ye this . . ." Time and weather had erased the rest. It did not matter. What words could ever encompass or even hint at the marvels of this world of pain and beauty?

I rang the bell that hung beside the door on a rusting chain.